Yellow Gentians and *Blue*

By

ZONA GALE

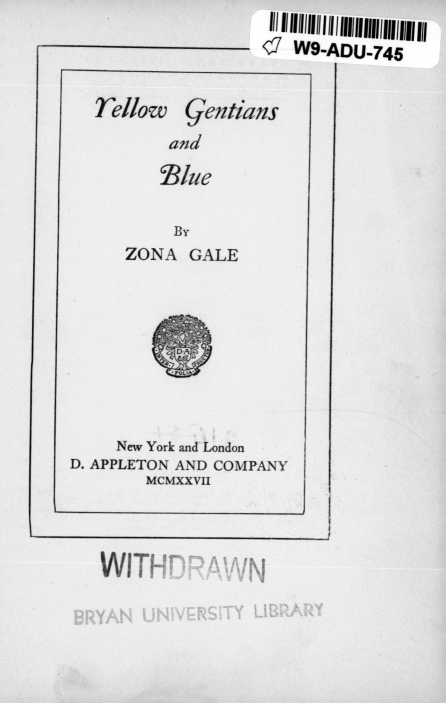

New York and London

D. APPLETON AND COMPANY

MCMXXVII

G
(Fiction)

21651

2099

Yellow Gentians
and
Blue

By ZONA GALE

CONTENTS

I

YELLOW GENTIANS

v

II

—AND BLUE

I

Yellow Gentians

. . . The yellow gentian which has a very bitter
taste.

NOAH WEBSTER

THE CHARIVARI

In one of the smallest farms in the Caledonia hills lived Obald Bronson, alone, and known down the countryside as the strange man who walked to the town to spare his one horse and who slept with no pillow. The people smiled at Obald when they met him walking to town. And he was so awkward and timid that they scorned him. Seven years before he had come among them from Norway, and that was all about him that they knew.

One day as a young Scotch farmer of the hills, Edward Muir, was driving a load of grain by Obald's house, he saw a little smoke curling from a window and when he ran in, calling and shouting, fire was eating at a wall and Obald was not there. It was a wood-box fire, no more, and Edward was able to put it out. He had never been in Obald's house and few of the Caledonia farmers had been there. He saw the room bare, neat, painted; food on the shelf, corn drying on a sunny board. Edward walked to the door of the inner room, wishing, or so he said to himself, to be sure that all was safe, and saw the bedroom, neat and tended and with no pillow, as they said. But it was the look of the third room which held him. For Obald, it seemed, had made for himself a parlor. He had a willow table, a willow chair, two painted chairs, a book, a china vase, and a new mahogany clock, ticking away. And under the window was a chest, whose walnut had been painted in wide orange bands so that, in the sun's reflection from the white wall, the stripes shone like gold. On the lid there was rudely painted a bird, blue and pale blue, and a large blue letter C.

Edward stood staring at this chest when Obald entered the kitchen.

"Neighbor," said Edward, "a little matter of fire brought me in here, but now I am staying because of this chest."

As Obald listened to an account of the fire

he said, "That was probably caused by my corncob pipe which must have fallen into my wood box." And then he grew greatly excited and cried: "But for you my chest might have been burned! What can I do for you that have saved my chest?"

So Edward Muir, who was young enough to have boy's curiosity and not old enough to be hypocritical, answered:

"You must not now talk of payment, but you can show me, if you like, what is in the chest."

At this Obald Bronson's face changed, he looked frightened, and on his forehead a red scar stood out which did not often show. Edward, seeing him so, cried: "But some other time, for my horses will not stand," and ran back to his grain, but not before he had seen the relief on Obald's face.

Edward told about the chest. He told his father, who thought that it must hold mementos; and his neighbors, who guessed papers or currency; and one wit who guessed bones. This man meeting Obald on the road, walking to save his old horse, cried out to him: "Obald! What is in your chest?"

Obald halted in his tracks and said: "What is that to you?" This tormentor made his look knowing and drove on.

Obald, who trusted every one, now had his door fitted with a lock, and set nails on his three windows. Now he went seldom to town, and when he went he rode the old horse, and rode him hard. One morning the animal was dead in the pasture. After that Obald was seldom seen on the road.

Because of this, and hearing from the locksmith about the new locks, the people talked the more, saying: "Either Obald is a miser or else. . . ." and shook their heads over him. Now, if they saw him, more than one cried: "Obald! We are coming to your house one night and find out a thing or two."

Such words he never answered. Only his face grew red and his scar showed. Then

they said: "Who knows how he came by that
scar?" Some asked him this question, and
laughed. They liked Obald, too, but he was
so timid and awkward.

Some boys of the neighborhood, having
heard the tales, came boldly one night and
rapped at the glass, crying. "Give us some
money. You've got lots of money!" Obald,
whom no man had heard in anger, shouted at
them to be gone, and so terrible was his voice
that the boys were charmed. It was then that
they said to one another:

"Let's cha'vari Obald."

This custom of the countryside offered to
the newly married was the highest form of
romance, next to love. So they prepared the
bones, combs, tin pans, the cowbell, and the
horse fiddle. And one midnight, gathered
about Obald's old house, they broke into such
wild turbulence and clangor that for miles
about the farmers heard the scraping, the
groaning and the shrieks.

But apparently Obald did not hear. He
did not come to the door or to a window.

This angered the boys, who had wanted no more than to torment him into giving them money for a drink, so they pounded on his door shouting: "Obald! Give us two dollars from your chest!" But still he made no sign.

For two days there was about the house no look of life. On the third day Edward Muir came with his neighbors, and they broke down the door. Obald was lying dressed on his bed, but not these men and not the coroner could tell how he had come to his death.

In his mail box a quarter of a mile down the road they found a letter, which had been there for three days. It was from Finmarken and they read:

When this comes to you, I shall be on the ocean. I will come straight to your town and you can meet me because I will send you a telegram. Oh, Obald—we have waited for seven years, and now the time that is so short seems so long. My love is the same—it is more, Obald.

CHRISTOPHA.

Then they knew the meaning of the things that they had found in the chest: the fan, the mirror, the silver chain, the linen, the cloth for a woman's dress.

AUTOBIOGRAPHY

"A swing under a fruit tree that seemed always in full bloom, some little dishes of pottery and a wooden doll—these gave me a happy childhood, at the hands of my parents, who were anxious but kind. I had a little schooling, not much, and then I worked in the mills and waited for the time to marry. That time came when I was nineteen and he was twenty-two, and we walked on the dike when the moon was big, and went to the fair with the others. We lived with my father and mother in the house where I was born, with the chard and melons of the garden meeting the creepers that grew over our front doorway.

"We should never have left the old country for we had it fine there. He was a ticket-taker in the Broadstone station, a good job he had, but his brother kept writing to him that America was the place to be and to make money. I says to him, 'You go then, and if you like it, I'll follow.' He was two years in America before he let on whether he liked it and then he didn't let on either, but he wrote to me to come over. It nearly killed me leaving my father and mother—for years I could see them as they looked when they said good-by—standing together on the flat stone, my father stiff and straight and my mother thinking the creepers covered up her crying.

"We had but the one little girl and she just big enough to run to meet me. She had eyes that never stopped their smiling, and yellow hair and a way that made strangers remember. That little thing and I, we came away together. But the big vessel was like a prison and the little one was frightened of the rolling and the pitching and she couldn't taste the food. The fifth day out she sickened—we'd a doctor on board, too, but he didn't know what that sickness was, made as it was three parts of fear and homesickness. The seventh day she died. That night they let me sit up beside her and the next day they came to take her away and I couldn't go up to see—I couldn't watch that thing they'd have to do. Then came a man of the ship who begged them to wait and he went down in the hold of the vessel and made a boatlike box, very small, and in that he laid my little one. Tender he was, like a woman. And he sealed her in, with narrow strips of the wood, and he made a sail of the sailcloth and fastened it on that strange boat. And when they'd let it down on to the water, they took me up to the deck. A little way off from the vessel it was by then—the tiny boat —rolling on the big waves, and it was sunset, so that the sail showed very white as the wind took it. So fast it went off over the water, so fast and so gay in the slanting sunlight. I watched it till the sun went, till the dark came and the little white dot went out. Then I went below. All the night in my closed eyes I saw her in the sealed boat, on the big water, her that I had tended and watched, and I kept remembering how frightened she'd been of the rolling and the pitching that was all the tending she had now. I couldn't stay in my berth and her out there, so I crept back up on deck again. And now the moon had come, and when I looked where I had left her, there was a sail in the far light—I know it was that sail I saw, and I watched till it died away again. Then I waited, looking toward where I knew it was, till the dawn came. When the dawn came there was only the gray water, empty.

"He met me at the boat, and I was alone, and then I had to tell him. But while I told him I saw he had something to tell me. He looked like a tramp—I had always seen him dressed as a ticket-taker or in his Sunday clothes. Now he was working as a day laborer at the wharf. He said: 'God forgive me for bringing you over, but I couldn't face it any longer alone.' I looked at him; I thought of my baby, dead of the voyage, and of my father and mother—so far away. But I looked at him, and I says, 'Where do we live, my dear?' He took me to two high rooms with no light. I sat there with a stone in my throat. But I didn't let on.

"I kept the two rooms tidy. I did all I could. The winters were hard, the summers were hard. In the fifteen years the four children came. In the fifty years since I've been in this country, they've grown to be men and women with homes to look after, and now they have grandchildren.

"Sometimes, sitting here in the Home where my four children pay out money to keep me comfortable, I think about them in their homes, where of course they can't bother with me. I think of him, that worked himself to death long ago; and of my father and mother that I never saw again. And of her in the little sealed boat with the sail.

"Life is like that for some of us—and yet we want to live, just like other folks."

BELNAP

FROM the moment that Alla went to work in the clubhouse, Belnap pursued her. She did all that she could to avoid him, but he would call her to his table and she dared not refuse the command of the head waiter. The head waiter was a woman of forty, a little lame, extremely capable, and kind to the girls. But when Alla explained to her why she wished to change from Belnap's table, this woman said to her, "You are a fool," and made no change.

Between Belnap's orders of expensive dishes, he would tell her how much he loved her and how instead of serving him she might now be sitting beside him at some other table, ordering filet mignon and parfait. Under her voice she would answer him sharply:

"Save your breath, Mr. Belnap." And aloud: "Shall your filet be brown or rare?"

"Rare. And Alla! I love you. I've a

little house in the country waiting for you. . . ."

"And it'll fall to pieces waiting for me. French dressing or mayonnaise, Mr. Belnap?"

"French. You little thing, I have never loved any one as I love you. I shall never love any one again as I love you. Alla, don't you understand. . . ."

By then she would have taken his order down and would turn her back.

Twice Alla gave up the place, but both times they sent for her to come back and as her father was ill and in want, she returned to the club where the wages were enough to pay for their two rooms, and the tips provided the food for her father and herself. No one was more generous with tips than Belnap and often she dreamed of all that she could do for her father if Belnap's purse were poured upon her, as he promised that it would be if only she would go with him to his little house in the country, among the apple trees. Also, he was an agreeable crea-

ture, and on the day when, between his order
for a salad of pears stuffed with cheese, and
his direction that there should be plenty of
Bar-le-Duc he said: "Alla! I will give you
a thousand dollars . . ." on that day she
hesitated for one instant and looked at him.
She saw the deep furrows between his eyes,
his cleft chin, his even teeth, and his look
already triumphant. "At what hour do you
finish here?" he breathed, but Alla cried quite
loudly: "I finish before you've finished, Mr.
Belnap," so that he looked about him in an-
noyance. Alla was balancing on the table's
edge a tray of empty dishes which she let
crash to the floor crying: "Now they will not
call me back here!"

On the death of her father she married a
clerk, and she lived for thirty odd years in
meager comfort. Her husband was by turns
kind and irritable, she was by turns patient
and complaining, and their two children were
by turns impish and angelic. The days were
a routine of cleaning and preparing for something which seemed never to come about.

Outside her house she knew that there were assemblages, disaster and stars, but these seldom concerned her, in the face of the needs of her children and her husband. All the days were the same.

At fifty, when her beauty was still marked, she heard from her doctor that the rich Mr. Belnap, now seventy, was living at a great hospital in the neighborhood. Her heart was kind and her life was humdrum, and so after brooding on the matter for days in the luxury of secrecy, she went secretly to the hospital and asked to see him.

Reading by a window in his brown bath gown, he looked handsome and ill. She saw the deep furrows between his eyes, his cleft chin, and his look, perpetually triumphant. Alla, the pleasant-faced dimpled woman, sat down before him and said: "Mr. Belnap, I want you to know that I have always thought of you kindly, for your tips brought my father many comforts. I am Alla, who waited on you at the City Club. Perhaps you do not remember. . . ."

His face lighted, he took her hand, he cried: "Indeed I remember. And you are still beautiful."

"But for you," she continued, "many necessities even would have been denied my father."

He lifted his hand. "But tell me," he said, "have you sometimes thought of me?"

"Yes—and only with gratitude."

He leaned toward her.

"And of the night when you first went with me into the country. . . ."

She searched his face. His eyes were dreaming beyond her. He said with a sigh: "I have never forgotten those weeks in my little house with the apple trees."

She sprang to her feet and cried: "Mr. Belnap, I am Alla—your old waitress at the City Club."

"Yes," he said gently, "you are Alla. Can you doubt that I remember?"

BILL

BILL was thirty when his wife died, and little Minna was four. Bill's carpenter shop was in the yard of his house, so he thought that he could keep up his home for Minna and himself. All day while he worked at his bench, she played in the yard, and when he was obliged to be absent for a few hours, the woman next door looked after her. Bill could cook a little, coffee and bacon and fried potatoes and flapjacks, and he found bananas and sardines and crackers useful. When the woman next door said this was not the diet for four-year-olds, he asked her to teach him to cook oatmeal and vegetables, and though he always burned the dishes in which he cooked these things, he cooked them every day. He swept, all but the corners, and he dusted, dabbing at every object; and he complained that after he had cleaned the windows he could not see out as well as he could before. He washed and patched Minna's little garments and mended her doll. He found a kitten for her so that she wouldn't be lonely. At night he heard her say her prayer, kneeling in the middle of the floor with her hands folded, and speaking like lightning. If he forgot the prayer, he either woke her up, or else he made her say it the first thing next morning. He himself used to try to pray: "Lord, make me do right by her if you see me doing wrong." On Sundays he took her to church and sat listening with his head on one side, trying to understand, and giving Minna peppermints when she rustled. He stopped work for a day and took her to the Sunday school picnic. "Her mother would of," he explained. When Minna was old enough to go to kindergarten, Bill used to take her morning or afternoon, and he would call for her. Once he dressed himself in his best clothes and went to visit the school. "I think her mother would of," he told the teacher, diffidently. But he could make little of the colored paper and the

designs and the games, and he did not go
again. "There's some things I can't be any
help to her with," he thought.

Minna was six when Bill fell ill. On a
May afternoon he went to a doctor. When
he came home he sat in his shop for a long
time and did nothing. The sun was beaming
through the window in bright squares. He
was not going to get well. It might be
that he had six months. . . . He could hear
Minna singing to her doll.

When she came to kiss him that night, he
made an excuse, for he must never kiss her
now. He held her at arm's length, looked
in her eyes, said: "Minna's a big girl now.
She doesn't want papa to kiss her." But her
lip curled and she turned away sorrowful, so
the next day Bill went to another doctor to
make sure. The other doctor made him
sure.

He tried to think what to do. He had a
sister in Nebraska, but she was a tired woman.
His wife had a brother in the city, but he
was a man of many words. And little

Minna . . . there were things known to her which he himself did not know—matters of fairies and the words of songs. He wished that he could hear of somebody who would understand her. And he had only six months. . . .

Then the woman next door told him bluntly that he ought not to have the child there, and him coughing as he was; and he knew that his decision was already upon him.

One whole night he thought. Then he advertised in a city paper:

> A man with a few months more to live would like nice people to adopt his little girl, six, blue eyes, curls. References required.

They came in a limousine, as he had hoped that they would come. Their clothes were as he had hoped. They had with them a little girl who cried: "Is this my little sister?" On which the woman in the smart frock said sharply:

"Now then, you do as mama tells you and

keep out of this or we'll leave you here and
take this darling little girl away with us."

So Bill looked at this woman and said
steadily that he had now other plans for his
little girl. He watched the great blue car roll
away. "For the land sake!" said the woman
next door when she heard. "You done her
out of a fortune. You hadn't the right—a
man in your health." And when other cars
came, and he let them go, this woman told her
husband that Bill ought to be reported to the
authorities.

The man and woman who walked into
Bill's shop one morning were still mourning
their own little girl. The woman was not
sad—only sorrowful, and the man, who was
tender of her, was a carpenter. In a blooming of his hope and his dread, Bill said to
them: "You're the ones." When they
asked: "How long before we can have her?"
Bill said: "One day more."

That day he spent in the shop. It was
summer and Minna was playing in the yard.
He could hear the words of her songs. He

cooked their supper and while she ate, he watched. When he had tucked her in her bed, he stood in the dark hearing her breathing. "I'm a little girl to-night—kiss me," she had said, but he shook his head. "A big girl, a big girl," he told her.

When they came for her the next morning, he had her ready and her little garments were ready, washed and mended, and he had mended her doll. "Minna's never been for a visit!" he told her buoyantly. And when she ran toward him, "A big girl, a big girl," he reminded her.

He stood and watched the man and woman walking down the street with Minna between them. They had brought her a little blue parasol in case the parting should be hard. This parasol Minna held bobbing above her head, and she was so absorbed in looking up at the blue silk that she did not remember to turn and wave her hand.

LAST NIGHT

In the scale house at the Junction it was dark and safe. It was quiet, save for the lowing of cattle in the yard. He swung down his peddler's pack and sat on that. From his pocket he drew the parcel that the tollgate woman had given him. He had not looked inside and here it was too dark to see what she had put into the sack. His fingers and tongue touched the soft substance—meat, cheese, he knew the tastes. Bread—and when he had finished, eating wolfishly as he did, he remembered that some of the bread had tasted sweetish. That must have been cake. He hadn't noticed.

He sat in the darkness. All day his body had felt heavy and dead, but he had pushed it about, with his one leg. This, now, was rest. This was a kind of home. Not like men's homes, but better than he had ever known, for he had known none. First he

had been a bound boy, then a hired man. He
had had a room over kitchens. For a summer or two he had tramped it, and slept in
groves or in straw piles or on the hay in barns.
But this place here, with no one about, was
the same as his own.

He had marked it one morning, crossing
the tracks near the stockyards, with his pack
of needles and pencils. The door had
yawned, open and friendly, and that night
he had come back, had watched, had slipped
inside. In the dry darkness he had slept,
undisturbed by the shifting trains. He had
slept here for many nights undisturbed, even
lulled by the lowing cattle in the little local
stockyard.

He lay down with his head on his pack.
He shifted his wooden leg so that it did not
hurt his knee. The lamps of the yard fell
in a white square on the wall and he looked,
feeling pleasure. Now, even if it rained, he
was safe. The place smelled of cattle, but
his clothes smelled horribly too, and he did
not notice either smell.

The tollgate woman's house had been clean. She had just finished giving her baby a bath. He supposed some one had washed him when he was a baby. Maybe not. He knew nothing about his life until he began himself to remember happenings—cuffs from the farmer, and the sharp voice of his wife. Except for swimming, he had washed but seldom in his life. The smell of cattle in the scale house did not bother him. And he liked to hear their lowing in the yard. He thought: "Company."

He had made forty cents that day. In his pockets were three dollars. Once he had had three hundred dollars, all at one time. He had paid it down on a fortieth of the farm owned by the man for whom he worked. The girl who had worked there had promised to marry him. She had laughed a great deal, but she had promised. He remembered that time the most often of all. But when the farmer's mortgage was foreclosed, they told him that he had no claim, and the girl had married a farm machinery agent. Emma.

She had been thick and pretty, like the toll-gate woman.

The tollgate woman had asked him three times whether he had erasers. He had been feeling heavy and dead and he couldn't think. She had looked at him as if he didn't know anything. He didn't know much. Two winters, wasn't it, at country school? He could write his name, but no one had asked him to write it since he could remember. He thought he could still make it—he thought how the letters went, imagined them in the square of light on the wall: Wm. Leeds. Curious that Wm. spelled William. Sometimes he had wondered who named him, but not any more. The tollgate woman had asked him his name and that at any rate he had answered quickly. "She smiled nice," he thought, and slept.

He lay inert, breathing. His body was as complex as that of any man. If he dreamed, he dreamed of the same things as another.

In the night he woke. A long freight train had rolled into the Junction and was drawing

noisily to a stop. Now rain was falling,
streaming from the eaves of the little build-
ing. He heard, dozed, felt warm and safe
and shut in. He wondered if this was what
men felt like at home. He thought: "At
home."

He came wide awake at the sound of cries
and clatter. A gate grated, the door of the
scale house was shoved open, a car door slid,
a man spoke angrily, there was the groping
muffled fall of many feet. Cattle were being
driven into the scale house. Outside a snarling voice protested that somebody was a fool,
and the answer was that the yard was full.
Cattle came blundering in.

Out there it was raining. He had no place
to go. Here it was warm and dry. He edged
to the little space back of the scales, held his
pack before his knees, waited. From the
doorway a lantern swung light over the
crowding dusky backs. They came in, as
many as the place could hold. The soft sides
were pressed close to the scales, the feet
trampled his wooden leg thrust stiffly out.

The snarling voice swore because no more could be crowded in there. The door slid and slammed.

The place was filled with the odor of the cattle—their untended flanks and their sweet breath. They moved and shouldered, lowed like lost creatures, tossing their heads. The place was full of the odor and movement and breathing of beasts. There was not room enough for them to lie down. They stood, restless, trampling, bewildered.

Wm. Leeds sat behind the scales and thought about the cattle. To-morrow they would have their throats cut. But they had some place to go, some one had sent them there, some one had paid for them and had taken money for them, some one was expecting them somewhere. His mind clung to that. Some one was expecting them somewhere. And if they had their throats cut, that was what they had been raised for. What had he been raised for? He had wondered about that. Here it was again. Even the cattle. . . .

Now, with the restlessness of the animals, he was unable to sleep. He heard them breathing, breathed with them, dozed, seemed to rise and fall on that strong breathing. They and he, safe and dry and shut in from the rain. But to-morrow they would do what was expected of them, while he. . . . Forty cents to-day. But what to-morrow? If it rained they didn't like you to track up the steps of their homes.

After daylight they came for the cattle, came crowding in, driving out those nearest the door—two men, harsh and sleepy. When they saw Wm. Leeds they swore. "The lock-up for you," said one. Wm. Leeds stood up stiffly—red, black, gray, brown, dirty.

"Look here," he said, "ship me on with the critters. Weigh me and ship me on."

The men, heavy, unshaven youths, stared at him. One, a wing of black hair in his eyes, jabbed at a cow with his elbow, struck it on a flank and said:

"Like to be butchered—eh?"

"Something," said Wm. Leeds.

The two men laughed loudly. "Go to the devil your own way," they told him magnanimously, and when the cattle were gone, they went away.

Now the scale house was foul and close. The man did not move from behind the scales. He felt heavy and dead. Down the yard he could see the cattle moving, leisurely, and with direction. They would be fed, watered, shipped on, butchered. Some one was expecting them. He dozed, feeling heavy and dead.

Toward night when some one came to clean out the scale house, there he was, grim and ugly to look at, heavy and dead. The yard man swore at the extra trouble. He was paid to take care of cattle.

The newspaper of the town whose name Wm. Leeds hardly knew, announced:

"The dead body of an unknown man was found in the scale house at the stockyards, where he had been making his home while he peddled needles and pencils about the

town.   He was apparently about seventy
years of age and had lost one leg."

He was buried by the town the next morning, not far from the time of the arrival of
the cattle train at the Chicago stockyards.
And the beef quotations were showing an
active market.

BELLA

THE Leels were the first family of Oderhill. For example, Mr. Leel might have consented to be pallbearer to any one in the
town, but only the very few could have been
invited to be pallbearer to Mr. Leel.

His monument was high, obelisk shaped
and white. He was laid beside his wife, and
there would be nobody else in the lot save
Bella. If Bella married as of course, with
her fortune, she would, then that smooth
green of clover would never be disturbed.

But Bella was secretly known in Oderhill
as queer. She was small, blue and white.
She said strange things. If she were to come
to some outrageous end, the town would say
that it had always known she would; but if
on the contrary she proved a person of distinction, then all would remember that they
had discerned distinction in her. Oderhill
could not understand her, but the family was

so rich that every one took her for granted.

However, when Mr. Leel's estate was settled, Oderhill was shaken. Nothing remained, save only his square brick house with the cupola and its old-fashioned furnishings.

Bella, who was now twenty-six, lived in the house and rented rooms to teachers. And the town, which had secretly found her queer, now saw her without the veil of the Leel wealth, and knew that she was queer.

Since she "entertained" no more, she was not entertained. She worked very hard and had time for few contacts. It became evident that Bella's life was to consist of renting rooms to teachers.

But she knew nothing about her occupation. She often thought that like boarding-house keepers and mothers, she was utterly untaught in her profession. From the first it was difficult for her to make her expenses. Shortly she was in debt.

A real estate man named Emmons Decker had opened an office in Oderhill, and one day he came to see Bella. He had wondered if

her house was for sale. She repudiated the
idea with something of the grand manner of
her mother. But this man was excessively
polite, treated her with great consideration,
said her name many times in direct address,
and Bella felt that she was being treated as
he had probably never treated any one before. So when he asked her to consider the
matter and to let him confer with her again
"on the proposition," she assented. He returned to confer, and more than once.

But about the sale she was obdurate. She
told him, often, who her mother and father
were and how well they were connected. She
showed him the silhouettes, the cameos, the
seed pearls and the Paisley. And the site was
desirable. In time Emmons Decker, with
his manner of great consideration, asked her
to marry him and she agreed. At the time
she wondered why, but as she made up the
teachers' four rooms the next day, she knew
why. And when the month's bills came in,
she realized that she could not have done
better.

Before they were married tax time came, and Bella confided to her fiancé that she had not the money to meet her taxes. Decker now said that frequently in their business they paid the taxes of others. It was a business arrangement, he said, when she permitted him to pay hers. Now he seemed in no haste to be married, business took him to the west, he returned toward tax time of the next year and again she permitted him to pay. Three times he did this during the engagement; and then he broke the engagement, invoked the state law in tax titles, took possession of the Leel house, and sold it.

Bella rented a room over a store. She was now thirty-three or four and without training for anything. The man who kept the store had no home, managed a makeshift home in the rear of his store. Bella's room was neat and comfortable, it had the Leel parlor curtains and a Leel lamp, and once when she cooked something savory from a can, she shared the meal with her landlord, who was lonely himself. He could not

afford to marry. In a little while Oderhill
was scandalized.

It now seemed incredible that she could be
Bella Leel—her clothes, her furtive walk,
her hair. All those who had felt her to be
queer were triumphantly justified, and those
who had thought that she was so queer that
she might amount to something, now thought
that there must have been bad blood in Mrs.
Leel. When the man left her, Bella sold
little things at the doors—dust cloths and
soap. In ten years Bella was the lost soul
of the town.

At fifty-five she was taken to the county
house and at sixty she died. And as they
were about to bury her in the county
cemetery, Emmons Decker, now a first citizen
of Oderhill, remembered the Leel lot and
the monument. There was no doubt that
Bella Leel had the right to be buried beside
her parents.

Decker and other first citizens conferred
concerning a funeral. No church could re-
ceive that clay. No home in Oderhill offered

it harbor. The little town had no funeral chapel. But there chanced to be an empty store in the main street, and they chose this. They seated it, spread down a rug, and brought in a victrola. At the hour of the service several who recalled the Leels were present, a retired minister preached about the woman at the well, and the victrola played "Beautiful Isle of Somewhere."

On the Leel lot, near the monument, obelisk shaped and white, the smooth green of the clover was disturbed to make her grave. There they laid Bella, at sixty, the lost soul of the town, beside the dust of her mother and father, of the first family of Oderhill. But Bella's grave has no headstone. They decided merely to carve her name on the obelisk.

CHERRIES

THE moon being very bright, Angus Sharp asked Nellie to drive to Wild Rose. It was already eight o'clock and she said that a bushel of cherries had just been delivered for canning, and her mother and she were to pit them that evening; but the next morning she could go. So Angus stayed and helped with the cherries. They all ate of the fruit, which was exceedingly ripe and red, though Angus said that Nellie's lips were redder and sweeter. It was not yet a fortnight since Nellie had promised to marry him.

The next day Albert Jolly drove down the street late in the afternoon, with his new trap, dark blue and shining. And Nellie was on the front lawn. So Albert stopped at the curb and leaped down, himself dark blue and shining, and asked Nellie to drive to Partridge for dinner. Partridge was only ten miles away, Nellie was tired from her day

with the cherries, there was in the house nothing good for dinner, Albert was an old
friend, and Nellie said that, providing she
could be back by eight o'clock, she would go.

The drive to Partridge was pleasant, but
there were detours, the dinner was delayed,
they met some friends, and when she reached
home the moon had risen, Angus had already
called for her, and had gone.

"I told him that you drove to Partridge
with Albert," said her mother. "Wasn't that
all right?"

Nellie sent for Angus the next morning
and tried to explain. She said: "You know
that there is nobody but you . . ." and
such things. But Angus was literal and he
said that there was Albert, too. She told
about the years down which she and Albert
had been pals, no more;—and Angus was not
comforted. And of how she had longed to
take the air after the fatigues of the cherry-
canning, and Angus said that he would have
taken her for the air. And of how proud
Albert was of his new trap—but as the

buggy in which Angus took Nellie about was
years old, Angus was unimpressed. He said,
and more than once, that they were engaged.
At last Nellie became annoyed, answered that
to be engaged was not to be deceased, and so
fell into silence. Before the evening was
finished their engagement was broken.

If in that consummation Nellie had no
sense of finality, this did not appear in her
voice or in her face or in her farewell. The
moon was shining brightly on the porch when
Angus went away forever. Nellie expected
him to call her the next morning, to arrive
the next evening. Because of her expectation
she even refused an invitation to a picnic in
Partridge. But Angus did not return.

He went straight to May Clinton. May
was large, pink and gentle. In his passionate
desire to show Nellie his indifference, Angus
asked May to marry him, and she consented.
The third moon from the time of cherries
shone down indifferently on May and Angus
for their honeymoon.

Angus and May lived in a frame house for

twenty years. He had never loved her, and
she had married him for a home. Her
placidity soon enraged Angus and he enjoyed
trying to make her jealous. He succeeded
very well. He would make a show of having received letters of whose contents he
would tell her nothing, he returned from
journeys and pretended to make mysterious
allusions; and at last he even talked sadly of
Nellie and openly called her his lost love.
May's gentleness grew stale, then acid, her
face sharpened and flattened and became
quilted with wrinkles and trails of tears.
Angus smiled at her, two rows of white teeth
gleaming through a black beard, and called
her "darling" and "treasure" in a tone of
unspeakable rancor. When their five children were still in school, he fell from the
roof of his barn, where he was trying to
rescue some young birds from a hawk, and
was instantly killed.

He left little property, May had none, and
the five children were taken out of school and
put to work. In a few years Elmer had be-

come a carpenter, Floyd a grocery clerk, Lucy a dressmaker, Amy had died of tuberculosis there in the village and Eloise had "run away" with a handsome man who sold swings.

May, the mother, grew sullen and bitter, remained indoors, closed the frame house against all visitors, took out her telephone, and lived on for twelve years like that. Before she died, Elmer, Floyd and Lucy were struggling to raise their own families of some size—Arthur and Annie, Jessie and Cora, little Angus, little May, little Elmer and the like. Lucy and her brood were under the roof of the frame house— "not large enough, really, for three generations," as Lucy said.

As for Nellie, at whose home the bushel of cherries had been delivered, she used to speculate on how it might have been if Eph, the express boy, had not brought that bushel basket to her mother until the next morning. But this she soon forgot for she married the chief banker of the town, had a beautiful home and an idiot son

THE PIECE

BILGER came home from town and turned into the narrow cement walk leading to his house. His daughter May was practicing at the piano, and the air which she played came to him through the open window. Over this window a grapevine grew on a little lattice, and beneath were lilacs. On a porch post there was a vine whose name he did not know and the vine had many flowers. Bilger stood for a few minutes looking at his house, listening to his daughter's music; and his heart filled with happiness.

The air which she played was not one which he had known, but he liked it. He beat time to it with his foot and his head. May was seventeen, but she was just beginning to "take," as the village denominated musical instruction, and Bilger had bought her a grand piano. He entered the house and listened by the hall door. She did not like to be disturbed.

"What was that piece you were playing?" he asked her at dinner.

"What piece?" she inquired and added proudly: "I play several."

"It went—*you* know—ta-ta, ta-ta-ta, up and down, kind of sad," Bilger explained.

She said: "Papa, don't be ridiculous."

But after dinner, when he asked her to play to him, and she played all the six pieces that she knew, she came inevitably to the one that he liked. At his insistence she played it over and over.

But he could not remember its name. And next time he asked her for it, calling it "that slow one that I liked—*you* know," May said: "Oh papa, I have so many pieces. And here is a new one."

Bilger and his wife and May were so comfortable in their little home, and Bilger was so proud of them and of his grand piano, that death seemed irrelevant. And when May fell ill and in ten days died, Bilger could not believe in his loss. His comfortable elderly wife was immediately convinced—for twenty

years she had looked for disaster and when
it overtook them she went about with an air
of resigned familiarity. But Bilger was
thunderstruck. He! And May! But above
all, *he!*

In the first day or two of her illness, when
she was still about the house, he had asked
May to play the piece. And she had done so,
with queer complaisance not in the least like
May. Every time that she played it she told
him the foreign name, which he said over—
with his own vowel values—and instantly
forgot.

Before May's funeral he said to her
mother: "Couldn't we have them at—*you*
know—the funeral—play that piece May
used to play—I guess you know the one."

She turned on him her solid-colored face,
with its flat mats of shadow beneath the eyes,
and said:

"I don't know what one you mean, but I'm
almost sure it wouldn't be suitable for the
funeral."

He said no more.

He missed May extravagantly. He had been to her a sealed father and she to him had been a sealed daughter; but he missed her.

It was not her virtues that he missed, nor her meanings, for the first he had but assumed and of the second he had no idea. However he missed her bobbed hair when she shook her head, and her whistle to the parrot, and her way of laughing with her eyes closed. And he missed the piece that he liked.

It seemed to him that if he could hear that piece played on the piano, he would have comfort, he would almost have May again. He turned all her music, but he himself knew not one note from another and to him all those sheets were dumb. He tried to make her mother know, but she said: "You remember I am not musical." He asked one of May's friends to play May's pieces for him, but none sounded like the one that he sought. This young woman said: "You'd have to sing

it better than that. It doesn't sound like anything, Mr. Bilger." Then he went to her
music teacher. To this distinguished organist
Bilger observed earnestly:

"It went—*you* know—ta-ta, ta-ta-ta—
kind of sad, but not all sad. It had one glad
part. And it went up and down."

"My dear Mr. Bilger . . ." said the
organist.

"It went like this," said Bilger, and sang
it, he thought.

"It must have been something that she
taught herself," her teacher suggested.

Then one day Bilger heard it on a street
piano. He could not be mistaken—there it
was, up and down, sad part, glad part. He
demanded of the street piano man the name
of that piece. The man hunched eloquent
shoulders, but for a quarter he played it over
and over again. Bilger stood on the curb and
whistled it, rushed home through the streets
whistling it, and appeared whistling before
his wife, and then shouted passionately:
"That's it—*you* know—that's the one."

But she said: "That doesn't sound like a tune."

"I'll have that piano fellow up here," cried Bilger, and rushed back to the spot where he had listened.

The street piano man, however, was gone. Bilger stood on the curb and tried to hear him on some other street, but he heard nothing. And when Bilger turned home again, comforted that now at least he could whistle that air, the air had left him. But he thought: "Sometime I'll get it back and whistle it to some of these symphony fellows. *They'll* know what it is."

THE SPIDER

THE little town is called Sunland and it lies in the mountains of the western United States. The circulars which came to the Iowa town said that Sunland was located on the richest soil of the warm areas of the Sierra foothills; that all fruits and vegetables would grow at a touch; that the climate was made by God and behaved as if it knew it; and that the land was cheap beyond dream— and within thirty days would be advanced in price to more than double the present cost. It was, the circulars concluded, an opportunity such as all America had never before afforded, and only a few localities were permitted to share in the prize. Would the reader of the circulars apply at once?

Matthew Pendleton read every word to his wife Liza. For years they had dreamed of California. Now they were sixty-four and sixty and if they were to make a change

it must be made soon. Bill Miller had gone
out alone and had grown rich on his lands.
They themselves were childless, they had
only themselves to risk, but the eighty acres
in the Iowa corn had been their home for
forty years. They had made grow with
their own hands the shed, the bay-window,
the porch. In the garden were strawberries
and asparagus and zinnias; there were an
orchard and a grapevine which yielded them
their preserves and jelly. Liza thought of
these things and said:

"We might go for only a little while and
see how we liked it."

"We must have the farm money to put
in the land, if we buy," said Matthew.

"We might go without buying first. . . ."

"The offer is for thirty days!"

She was silent. She looked at his hard
hands. "Do as you think best, Matthew,"
she said at last.

It was early spring and the crop was not
yet planted. There was no difficulty in sell-
ing the eighty acres, though Bart Mellon had

tried this long time to sell his farm and could not do so. Their furniture was old and they sold that too. Only Liza kept certain things and packed them in her trunk—her meat chopper, her cherry pitter, her aluminum kettle, and her two glass pie plates. And just before the men came for the auction, she suddenly wheeled to the side porch the plush couch and the plush chair and put with them the large colored Beatrice Cenci, whose name she did not know. Then she ran down the road to Bart Mellon's and asked their boy to come with his cart and set these things in his father's barn.

"We were fixed nice, Matthew," she said, as the last of the belongings were taken away by their new owners.

"Yes," said Matthew, "but think of how nice we're going to have it."

"Maybe," said Liza.

The tourist train was to them luxury. The journey was even better than motion pictures, Matthew thought. They ate from their basket, listened to every one, hardly spoke all the way across the desert, and looked everywhere with shining eyes.

"See, Liza, how nice we have it," Matthew sometimes said.

"Maybe," said Liza.

They reached Sunland at noon in the blazing blue and yellow of the western spring. They went down the street, slowly, for they could not breathe easily any more when they walked. Under the ferny acacias they made their way to the land office. There a spidery man with curved legs and a stiff neck called to a lounging boy to take them to their land. The lounging boy, with a manner of indifference amounting almost to unconsciousness took them in a neat car.

Under the acacias and the pepper trees, by the live oaks and the eucalyptus they drove at such speed that they were terrified and saw nothing.

"Here's the land," said the boy, when he stopped the car.

He waved his hand to ten acres lying up,

up the steep green foothills. It was per-
pendicular land.

"I don't understand," said Matthew.
"They said rich land . . ."

"None richer," said the boy, and tried to
yawn, but missed it.

The man with the curved legs and the stiff
neck later pointed out to them that all the
statements of the circular were true. And
they were true, literally true.

All night Matthew and Liza talked. "We
can put up a cabin on the strip by the road,"
Matthew said, "and spend the summer. We
got our pride."

"We can go back and buy Bart Mellon's
farm," said Liza.

In the sudden Sierra dawn he looked at
her, lips parted, and said nothing.

As they drove from the station to Bart
Mellon's farm a fortnight later, Matthew
said:

"Now we begin all over, where we were,
forty years ago."

"No, Matthew," said Liza. "We got a

plush couch, a plush chair, a picture, my meat chopper, my cherry pitter. . . ."

"We'll have it quite nice again," said Matthew.

"Yes!" cried Liza.

The man with the curved legs and the stiff neck bought offices in other towns and continued to do a brisk business.

VOICES

MILLY was fifteen years old when she went to work for Mrs. Pettigrew. The house was large and beautiful, and there were several servants, all highly specialized; and Milly's job was to do all the things which they refused to do. When in the spring the chamber maid refused to bring down the wicker furniture from the storeroom because the verandah was the care of the parlor maid; and when the parlor maid said that the storeroom was on the second floor and out of her hands, then Milly brought down the wicker furniture. But the work was pleasant, for she helped them all, on three floors and in the basement, and had not the burden of deciding whether this was her job or that, for she was engaged to do anything.

One morning Mrs. Pettigrew ordered Milly to select some old garments from a certain trunk. The sharp tone of her mistress was Milly's chief dismay; and when she would be happily at her work, and the sharp thin tone would come ordering her, Milly would tremble, and at the back of her head there would flicker a fiery pain. She longed to say, "Please, please do not speak to me so," but she dared not, having been so highly recommended by her agency. She went now to the attic and selected the old garments, as the sharp voice bade, and brought them to the limousine waiting at the door. Seated beside her mistress in the blue velvet lined car, Milly was glad of the beauty and the bearing of Mrs. Pettigrew, of her perfumes and her gown.

They took the old clothes to the workhouse for two women who were to be released, a mother and her daughter. Mrs. Pettigrew and Milly saw them, spotted and underfed and defiant. The daughter said openly that if it had not been for her mother, she should not have been where she was; and when the older women ordered her raucously, "Shut up, Little Varmint," the girl wept. But they both thanked Mrs. Pettigrew quite nicely for the serge suits and the hats with ornaments.

"What are they going to do now?" Milly asked, as the limousine rolled away.

"How on earth should I know?" Mrs. Pettigrew cried sharply.

"I was wondering," said Milly.

With mounting irritability Mrs. Pettigrew said that they had not asked her what *she* was going to do and she saw no reason why she should ask them. And her voice was so hard and sharply edged that Milly felt fear and a physical nausea.

In a little time, a matter of months, it became clear that nearly everything Milly said irritated her mistress. Milly was pink and full, like a dahlia, and pretty, too. But she spoke with so enormous a distinctness. She would say loudly and nakedly in the hearing of others: "Shall I cut off the buttons?" before an old gown was to be sent to some one; or, "Is the yesterday cake good enough for tea?" And when she had her reply she in-

variably added: "I was wondering. . . ."
At last everything that she said annoyed Mrs.
Pettigrew, who would answer her with a
strangled irritation as sad as violence. And
the arrows in the tone of her mistress pierced
Milly, set her to trembling, gave her the fiery
pain flickering at the back of her head and a
great weight on her chest.

One evening Mrs. Pettigrew said to Milly:
"Take down the rose gown and give me the
silver brocade slippers."

"The old slippers?" Milly asked, with
enormous distinctness.

"Certainly *not!*" cried Mrs. Pettigrew,
jarred and mangled not by the words but by
their pitch.

"I was wondering . . ." said Milly
trembling.

Mrs. Pettigrew rose from her dressing
table. She too was trembling. She spoke in
a terrible voice:

"Milly, I cannot stand it. Your voice
drives me frantic. You'll have to go. I give
you your notice. You'll have to go!"

"Yes'm," said Milly. "How much is my notice? A week—yes'm. I was wondering. . . ."

Mrs. Pettigrew did not pry into Milly's affairs. Milly had no home. Work was scarce. In six weeks she had used her savings. The demands of society faced her: shoes, a winter coat, food. A man said: "I'll be your friend." These words seemed beautiful to Milly until she understood. But she was ill and hungry and despised by Mrs. Pettigrew, and she had read in Mrs. Pettigrew's books that such friendships happened. She went with him.

As the years passed, and other such friendships followed, she ran the gamut of the garden—from dahlia, ripe with summer, to frowsy autumn-flawed chrysanthemum.

At forty she was nearing the end of a sentence in the workhouse when a lady came to her cell. This lady had now a face like an eagle, but Milly knew her winter beauty, her bearing and her perfume.

"My poor woman," said Mrs. Pettigrew

kindly, so kindly, "what brought you here?"

"I lost my job," Milly answered.

"Yes? Well? Go on . . ." Mrs. Pettigrew pressed her. "I meant, you know, in the first place. . . ."

"I lost my *job*," Milly repeated.

"But what else?" Mrs. Pettigrew encouraged her sharply.

Her tone set Milly to trembling in the old way. From out the perfect anonymity of her battered face, Milly answered:

"It was on account of my voice—my voice. . . ."

As Mrs. Pettigrew left, she said to the attendant: "The poor thing—had she, then, been a singer?"

They were interrupted by Milly calling loudly down the corridor her forgotten thanks for the suit which Mrs. Pettigrew had brought, and the hat with an ornament.

THE BLUE VELVET GOWN

My mother and I used to walk, in the mornings, in a pleasant valley near our home, and we would stop at a cottage where lived a woman who did our laundry work and who often told my mother her story. And I remember everything she said though this was fifty years ago.

Blue velvet, she said, became her best, and it was blue velvet that she was wearing when she broke the seal of Barlo's letter. He wrote a hard hand, biting into the paper: Might he see her for only a moment on a matter most important to himself. "I am not known to you, I take care of the harnesses in the coach house, and sometimes I have brought round the horses. But do not refuse this. . . ." She told the messenger that she would come to the south terrace in an hour, as the letter asked.

Sitting through the long dinner with the

other ladies-in-waiting to the old princess, and with the gallants of the little court, she wondered what this stranger should have to say to her, he whose writing was so savage and bit so deep into the page. She looked at the white hands of the little lord beside her, heard the fulsome praise and pretense of the others, saw the old princess doze, and she scorned them all. Of the ladies in silver and rose she thought: "Who has ever asked aught of you?" When they called her to the harp-sichord, she escaped them and stepped to the south terrace as the moon was rising red, above the thin young trees. The castle lay long and dark, its hundred windows shrouded, by moving creepers, from the moon.

In a full play of the moonlight he was waiting, and he came toward her, and his voice ate its way into her as his writing had scored the page:

"I am in danger. I leave here to-night. It is because of the things that I believe make a man's freedom. These many months when

I have brought the horses round, I have read
your face. I have a young sister. I would
beg you sometimes to see her—to let her
sometimes be with you. . . ."

"You leave England? You go. . . ."

"To America. Where a man may think
his thoughts."

Beyond the belief of any one he was beautiful, tall, strong, possessing. She looked up
at him, saying nothing while he talked much
of freedom and his hatred of courts. But
his words faltered, and she being so fair, and
he so near, suddenly he stooped to her hand
and whispered: "God forgive me, I lied. I
think that my sister is safe enough. The
truth is that I wanted once to see you near—
and alone. Now I can ask no more. . . ."

He began, but not with his eyes, to take
leave of her; and since this was good-by, abruptly he told her of his old passion for her,
of how she had long sung in his being, how
he had watched outside the hundred windows for her face. He was like no other
man, he with his soft ways, his bigness, his

biting eyes, and his rough clean clothes. The
little philandering lords within the castle
were a weariness; and before this man crying
out to her but with no words, she held her
bright head like a sudden banner, and she
said: "Why do you not ask me to go with
you. . . ." as a man might have spoken in
those days. In that moment she was in his
arms. He whispered: "If I do not escape
those men who love not freedom . . ."
and even: "There is a price upon my head."
But she was in his arms and she answered:
"You *shall* escape them. I can answer for
that."

When he strode away in the moonlight,
then returned and lingered and drove himself from her side, she said to him that for
this she had lived her life.

When the two sailed on a tramp steamer,
she had with her all the gowns and trappings
that she had worn at the court of the old
princess, together with hose and underthings,
silken and pale, slippers of silver and gold,
and many ornaments of French paste. He

asked only that she bring the blue velvet
gown that she had worn that night on the
terrace.   Thus she left her people—her
mother, father, home.

On the ship Barlo owned to her that he
had no sister. "I meant to bring you with
me," he boasted.

They lived far inland in America, where
the pioneering was yet in progress, and ways
were wild.   Barlo made with his own hands
a rude home, she did what she could to keep
it neat and warm, but it was little and bare.
Instead of plate and flowers there were tin
and oilcloth; and there was water to fetch
from the spring and wood from the pile at
the clearing's edge.   She bore and raised children—six that lived, children who loved
beauty and saw none but the beauty of the
wilderness and the sky with its yellow wilds
of light.   At night Barlo would come home,
cast down his ax, and stretch out by the fire;
and their talk would be of grain and hides
and the beasts in the shed.

Once when she told him that a stranger

had come asking for him, he turned a queer
solid-color, so that she cried out: "*Was* it for
the freedom of your thought that a price was
on your head?" But his eyes and his voice
bit into her so cruelly that she never asked
again. Yet in his own overpowering fashion
he loved her; and to her all nights might
have been as that first night, on the south
terrace.

While yet the children were little, a letter
came to him, brought by a messenger riding
hard, and she seeing his stress broke the seal
and read. Thus from that morning she knew
why indeed Barlo had been forced to leave
England. She sent the messenger away with
food in his wallet, resealed the letter, met
her husband with her smile, asked nothing,
and even turned away while he read. Nor
after the reading did she let a questioning
silence fall, but spoke casually of the beasts
in the shed.

When now in haste he changed their
dwelling place, and went driving west and
camping by the way, she acquiesced with no

question. When she saw him build in the
new cabin a wood box of logs, and having a
part where a man might lie, she seemed not
to notice. She lived beside him, saying not
a word of what she knew.

Now they were come among the mines, to
a place rougher and wilder than before, and
she would sit through the evening, watching
her children at their books. For they grew
and loved beauty, and they had none to see.
So one day, in her husband's absence, she took
the children into her bedroom and spread before them those gowns and trappings which
she had brought with her from overseas—the
blue velvet and the gold and silver cloth, the
colored hose and the slippers, and the ornaments of French paste. Sitting in the
kitchen with its one window toward the dense
wood, she told them of the house in which
she had lived, whose hundred windows were
shrouded, by creepers, from the moon.
"And the summer palace had a window for
every day in the year," she told them
proudly. The children listened, slender

aristocratic things, the girls like lilies, the
boys like blades. Then all the eyes in the
kitchen dreamed of beauty.

Barlo too dreamed, but he muttered in his
sleep, woke crying out in fear, and he began
to speak to her with oaths. To forget his
deep shadows, he brought strong liquors
from the town. He grew afraid to venture
out, he sat all day by the stove; he sent his
children for the liquor. At this she remon-
strated, and he snarled, and struck her.

One night when the food was eaten and
there was nothing for her to cook, she put
on her blue velvet gown, the silver slippers,
and her ornaments on her shoulders and her
arms, and she came and sat by Barlo, before
the kitchen range. He looked at her and
burst into weeping, rose and overturned a
chair, cursed, and flung out of the house.

She stood in the kitchen doorway and
watched him go. The moon shone above the
thick black of the wood, and surged on the
little kitchen, with its single window bare.
She saw him stride away, his feet biting into

the trail, his body boring into the dark.   She
did not see him again.

When it became clear that he would not
return, she moved their few belongings
nearer to the little town where she could sell
her butter and eggs.   But there was not
enough for the seven mouths, and she began
to do laundry work for the well-to-do of that
place.   On the wall of the General Store she
advertised: "Monica St. Mount, laundry."
It was so that she contrived to send all her
children through the school of the town.
Then they went out, one by one—somewhere
in America—to find beauty; all save the
youngest, a lordly girl, who stayed to help
her mother.

One morning when my mother and I had
walked across our pleasant valley and stopped
at her door, we found this young daughter
on the door step.   At once she explained without emotion: "My father has been arrested.
He had gone back to England.   We have
just heard that he is there, in gaol."   Me-
chanically my mother protested his inno-

cence, but the child said no, quite quietly; and in a voice of incredible maturity she named his crime. I remember how my mother paled, and the little girl led us to the tiny kitchen.

There, over her tubs, Monica St. Mount toiled, and at our entrance she glanced down at herself with an apology.

"You must forgive my costume," she said, "I've really nothing else to wear, any more."

She was washing her clothes, in the soap and the steam, and wearing a blue velvet gown, richly trimmed in the fashion of a bygone day.

TOMMY TAYLOR

When Aunt Parmenter Taylor was dying, she said something which nobody could distinguish, and she died with the words locked by her lips. So her favorite nephew, Tommy, who had hoped to inherit some of her property, got nothing but the cherry chest of drawers which she had always said that he must have. He now had nothing with which to finish the home that he had begun to build while Aunt Parmenter's cancer was yet in its first stages.

From nine black windows and one black door Tommy's cream brick house looked over Belle Prairie—a shell of a house, its two great parlors, its dining room, its library and its four "chambers" standing within their outer walls and their lath. But the kitchen was finished and two low bedrooms and a loft overhead, and for six years the family had lived there: Mr. and Mrs. Taylor, Lucien, Amy and Jane.

Every time that Tommy went to the town, he heard the people say: "Wonder when Tommy'll get his house done."

Every time that Mrs. Taylor went to church she heard the women whisper: "No signs of the house being finished yet, is they? Beulah Taylor, she won't lord it over us yet awhile."

And at dances, the young folk said boldly to Lucien and Amy and Jane: "Hurry up and get your house done, why don't you, so you can have a housewarming."

These gibes the Taylors took variously: Amy and Jane with secret tears but unabated hope; Lucien sullenly so that his birthmark looked purple; Tommy's wife with a head held high in public, an appearance of cheerful expectation before her friends; and toward her husband a neutrality in peace, but an occasional piercing thrust in moments of domestic dissonance. It was Tommy himself for whom the situation was both dart and poison. For though he was gentle and hopeful, yet when his crops failed for the fourth time, when investments stood still, when he faced a fifth winter behind the nine black windows and the one black door, he became unbearable about the house, and gave his family to understand that this ill luck was in some direct way traceable to them. So his wife said placidly: "That may be—since we've a husband and father not like other folks." Then they had a black hour—Amy and Jane, pink, white and golden, feeling the need of golden feathers to match; and Lucien, who said that he was sick of being the joke of Belle Prairie, and flung out of the house, his birthmark glowing.

Now Tommy pulled down the burlap which they had hung over the door of the embryo dining room, and he stalked alone through his naked rooms, large and lordly, high, and set with the hollow threats of fire-places. Here he had dreamed of entertaining his neighbors about a freighted table; in the "study" were to have been ranged rows of bright books, and there he had meant to keep his accounts, which now he had in the back of the almanac. He tiptoed, as he always did in here, across the rough flooring awaiting its hard wood in the two vast parlors. It was twilight and from within these rooms the windows seemed like soft faces pressing from the outside upon his walls, and mocking him for his ineptitude. And his two hundred and forty acres waiting about the unfinished house which they had failed to promote, lay like dust whereon he had breathed in vain. Tommy Taylor, the gaunt brown man, with the carriage of a gentleman and a telltale looseness of wrist and indecision of gesture, stood up and beat with his fist on the top of Aunt Parmenter's cherry chest of drawers which was indeed the only bit of furniture in the rooms on which a man could beat his hands, if he wanted to.

"I'm damned," he said aloud, "if I can keep on like this."

He unbolted the wooden door over the aperture which was to have been his front entrance, swung himself loosely down from the high lip of the threshold, and entered the night. At Belle Prairie the hotel keeper lent him a little money; he made his way to the city a hundred miles away, and from there notified his family that he was going west. "I shall make the money to finish the house, or . . ." he wrote, and wrote no more. And though he wrote inconclusively, and they thought that he would be back in a few days, he did not return.

Tommy Taylor stayed in the west for seven years. Meanwhile Lucien ran the farm, and made no more than would hold together the four souls and the four bodies. And this was tragedy, for there was Bethna, who waited for Lucien through those seven years, and would not come into the little kitchen to live with his family—no, not even if he finished off one of the chambers, as he hoped in time to be able to do. Amy and Jane reached their late twenties, and pink and white and golden though they were, not a boy on the prairie asked them in marriage. For none of the boys, presumably, cared to be drawn into that great cream brick web, looking so hopefully from its nine eyes for somebody to come and share the heavy burden of itself. There were Dan and Harvey, who "shone round," Belle Prairie said, longer than the others, and at last went off to the county seat and married school teachers. And after that Amy and Jane dropped out of the dances and seldom went in town. Mrs. Taylor was rarely seen, working as she did early and late in the kitchen and the lean-to, the spring house, the smoke house and the chicken yard, littered behind the rearing walls of her potential home. If sometimes driving home in the buggy back of the old gray, she dreamed her old dream of the pair of grays which should come pacing up the maple drive to a comfortable porch, she said nothing, and merely alighted, a broad-backed shabby woman, at her kitchen door. But when she met her neighbors, she held her head high: "Good news from Mr. Taylor—yes. But he'll not be back for another year. No, we shall do nothing about the house till he's here."

Seven years, Amy and Jane were thirty, Lucien thirty-two, their mother toward sixty. Now the eaves of the house were showing their lack of paint, the shingles had mangy spots, and burdock and Bouncing Bet were netted before the front door. Walking at twilight under the apple trees about the house, the women heard passers say: "Tommy Taylor's Folly."

Then, on a Saturday when the streets of Belle Prairie were filled, there he was back, shaking hands with every one. Tommy Taylor, gentle and pleasant and glad. And when had he looked so prosperous, so distinguished, so well-dressed, so well-shod? His hands were loose-wristed and wandering as always, but his eyes were so clear and so hopeful, his carriage so erect, and his coat so well-pressed that Belle Prairie said at its supper table: "Tommy Taylor's come back, to finish his house."

At his own supper table, Tommy Taylor

was being served to a spring chicken perfectly fried; and he was saying quite gently:

"No, I haven't got near enough to finish it, and I never would have had if I'd stayed there for forty years. But I've come to see that I've got a pretty good thing in this farm—no reason why I shouldn't make it pay now and go on with the house, in a year or two. Once . . ." he eyed his wife dreamily, "once I thought of investing in a fruit farm out in the Bitter Root and sending for you and the children. I could see a fortune, right there. But I guess I can make the farm go now, if we all turn in—and then, in a year or two, we'll finish the house."

At this Lucien, his son, began to laugh—flung back his head until his neck was long, and laughed very loudly, looking at the ceiling. After a moment of struggle, Amy and Jane joined him, and the laughter of the three, which should have been young laughter, free and wild, came from them shrill and gusty, like winds angry and not at play.

"The damned house," said Lucien. "Damn it, damn it. . . ."

He rose and caught the lamp and strode toward that door with its mock portière of burlap, and the girls sprang up and followed. "No, children, no, no, no . . ." said the mother feebly, and followed after them—her children in the thirties, laughing and laughing through the empty rooms, with the red glass lamp held high. And Tommy Taylor followed too, looking distinguished and prosperous and bewildered, his hands making wavering gestures as he went through that dining room where no neighbors came, that study in which he had no accounts to keep, and those parlors on whose walls the windows laid their faces, like something from without.

Lucien shouted: "It's killed mother. It's robbed the girls. It's done for Bethna and me—and what has it brought you? You're a hopeful old man. . . ."

The red lamp tipped, and his mother took it from him as she would have taken a danger from a child. And Lucien, standing as he was by Aunt Parmenter's cherry chest, his birthmark red and twisted, flung up his arm and brought it crashing down on the chest's flat top.

Something slid and thudded, dropped so sharply to the floor that they all looked down. The bottom of the chest had fallen out, and from under the lowest drawer a shallow drawer lay tipping. It was Mrs. Taylor who drew it out and saw lying there, unwrapped, piles upon piles of neatly folded greenbacks bearing the heady yellow design of gold certificates.

"Tommy!" she said.

They squatted about the drawer and the red lamp on the floor. They lifted the piles, ran them through, estimated—twenty-two piles wide, ten rows deep, twenty twenty-dollar bills in a pile. . . . It was Mrs. Taylor who whispered capably:

"Eighty thousand dollars."

"Aunt Parmenter," said Tommy, tensely,

"Aunt Parmenter. She tried to talk when she was dying. . . ."

They squatted about this drawer which for twelve lean years had kept vigil in the cherry chest, that single waiting piece of furniture in the empty house, that lordly and empty and naked house behind whose walls the family had starved and watched.

Like a coffin they bore the drawer among them into the kitchen, and there hid their treasure under the cupboard, and threw over it pieces of old carpet. Then they sat about, still whispering.

"We'll pay off old Matthews," said Lucien, "And Bethna and I'll start somewhere else."

"We'll finish the house," cried his mother, a deep breath waving her voice like ripe grain. In her eyes the rooms now spread warm, lighted, filled with neighbors, and she drove up to the door of her home behind a pacing pair, caught herself at that old dream, and came in a motor car.

Tommy Taylor's eyes were bright and

deep. His loose-wristed hands he smote
sharply together. "We'll sell the house to
Matthews," said he, "and your mother and
I will take this money, and go out to the
Bitter Root, and get that fruit ranch, and
start over again!"

For the space of a breath Amy and Jane
looked at each other. There could be no
starting over for them. Tommy's wife
stared at him, from out the sixteen years of
weariness and waiting that lay behind her
and from under a lifetime of weariness and
loss that formed on the air.

Then those sixteen years burst and blew
upon the room, and scattered their fragments
of hope deferred and dead. Amy and Jane
spoke with the bitter voices of the lovers
who had not asked them in marriage and
with the wail of children never born. No
journey for them toward the fruits of the
Bitter Root, and no finishing of the house;
but instead the chance to leave that farm
with enough of Aunt Parmenter's money to
keep them in the town while they found their

work.   Their   father   thundered   weakly:
"What is it you want there?"   Jane's lips
moved soundlessly, Amy cried out: "Some
life!"   And by this they now meant such
work as they could do—some sewing and
pickling for other women.

So with a few hundreds in greenbacks the
"girls" went away to the town.   With a
share of that treasure, Lucien married
Bethna and went out to make his way.   But
Tommy, who was weak to the world, was
iron to his wife.   A fruit ranch, he showed
her, was the place to make money, and they
would build another house better than this.

Though she talked bitterly and incredu-
lously, yet when Matthews, who held
the mortgage, took over at last the great
shell of their home, Mrs. Tommy Taylor
told her neighbors: "Yes, the children have
their plans, but Mr. Taylor and I are going
west.   He has found such a splendid open-
ing out there that we just can't afford not
to take it."

To "the children" she said: "I'll go with

him—yes. If we should separate and I should get along and he shouldn't, I couldn't stand that."

The house was finished by the new owner, whose motor car came and went under the maples, and the nine windows and the door continued to stare indifferently out upon Belle Prairie. Tommy Taylor loose-wristed, prosperous-appearing, hopeful, went west, looking for a ranch.

ERNIE MENDENHALL

ERNIE MENDENHALL was now forty-two years old, and still he had found no one with whom to share his home. His home was a white house in the town of Oderhill, and its little garden had fine hollyhocks. For four years, since the death of his parents, he had lived there alone, and in those four years he had bought now and then a piece of old furniture or a rug or some small article for his house. Every time that he did this, the neighbors would say:

"Ernie Mendenhall must be going to get married."

But so far he had not married. He earned his living as part-time secretary for a writer who lived on the edge of town. Every morning the neighbors saw Ernie's long form, swinging its right arm and holding its

Best Stories of 1926; Edward J. O'Brien (Dodd, Mead & Co.).

left arm stiff as it hurried along, his lips
moving in imagined talk. And they said:
"What can he be talking about, to himself
that way? He hasn't any business of his
own to reckon up."

One summer week-end the writer had a
house party for Alla Vintrin. On Sunday morning she walked into the library
where Ernie was working. He saw her frail
beauty in its pink linen enclosure, her
delicate profile, her heavy hair. The linen,
the profile and the heavy hair attacked him
as an epidemic attacks, and he was as one
who catches cold—instantly and pervadingly.

She said: "Is the old secretary in
this room—the Governor Winthrop secretary? . . ."

"Here," said Ernie with immense difficulty, and bowed, and perceived that he had
bowed not to her but to the secretary.

He managed to talk to her about that
piece of old mahogany. Afterward he wondered whether he had not perhaps said: "It
has a beautiful profile, heavy hair, and it

wears pink." And though he tried in agony
to recall her words, he could recover nothing save an assent, a murmur, a perfume.

Next he noted, from a great distance, that
he was saying to her, "if she was interested
in old furniture, he had some good pieces
in his house, if she cared. . . ." And she
said alertly that she did care, and could she
see them that morning? With no more
thought of the writer than of an eagle on a
far cliff, Ernie walked out of the house and
down the streets of Oderhill, and beside
him she went.

She said little—he liked her for that.
She walked rapidly—that he liked. She
was not so tall as he, she observed the flowers, she stopped and spoke to a child—she
was perfect.

Thanking God for an upbringing which
had forced him to keep order in his house,
he opened his front door and let her in upon
the hook rugs, the cherry chairs, and the
one piece of rosewood. It was before this
melodeon of rosewood that Alla Vintrin

paused at last, then sat, pulled out the stops, and pressed from the reluctant instrument its few remaining tones.

And at the sound of music, played by her, in his home, Ernie's years of waiting cried from his throat these words: "Could you stay? Could you live here? Could you be my wife?" And this he did not hear himself saying from a distance. No, for he was in the very words themselves.

She looked round the room, small, sweet and colored, and at the hollyhocks motionless beyond the glass. "Why not?" she said.

"You could? You would?" He was not sure that he said this at all. And all that he heard her say was "Why not?" as she moved to the door. He walked beside her under the maples, and told her about his life. Always he had wanted to tell somebody about his life, but when he had tried, his confidante had looked at him. Eyes could be puzzled, amused, disdainful. Alla did not look at him. She merely walked beside him and listened. "Could you?

Would you?" Ernie cried when he had
done.

"Why not?" she said again, with immense
sadness.

In the corridor at the writer's house she
gave him her hand, saying only: "I shall see
you again, Mr. Mendenhall—this afternoon,
perhaps."

But that Sunday afternoon all the house
party decided to motor back to town. Ernie,
who had made his task last into the day,
heard them go, saw them go, and sat at his
desk mute and blind.

Three days later he had a note from
Alla.

. . . and I know exactly how you are feeling
because you spoke so. I have asked one or two
men to marry me and wished afterward that I
hadn't spoken. But you mustn't mind. Those
forty-two years in Oderhill—you are likely to ask
anybody, anywhere. . . . I did mean to speak to
you about the melodeon. I assume that those
things are for sale, and if the melodeon is at all

within my reach I would like very much to buy
it. . . .

Every day the neighbors saw Ernie's long
form as it hurried along, his lips moving in
imagined talk with some one. He was writing to Alla Vintrin, composing his letters as
he walked the streets. He was telling her
of his life, its routine, its emptiness. These
letters he dared to write out. When her
bread-and-butter letter came to the writer,
Ernie copied the address, and it burned on
his bureau. One night, when it rained, he
took out his letters to her, read them over,
selected the mildest, addressed it, carried it
in his pocket for days. One day when he
had an influenza, he plucked the letter from
his pocket and mailed it.

As soon as the letter was mailed, he
fashioned her reply, many replies. She
would be kind, she would be cold, she would
be cruel. All these replies he wrote in his
mind. When days passed and no reply
came, he said to himself that she had gone

abroad. And when his letter reached her, at some lonely foreign place, how touched and warmed she would be that he had remembered. He thought that she would write: "My dear friend, you move me greatly." Once he had taken down that sentence, dictated by the writer: "My dear friend, you move me greatly." No answer came, but when he was at home for a week with lumbago, he chose another of his letters to her and mailed that. It required a call-ing-down by the writer and his omission from an Oderhill wedding reception to bring the third and fourth letters to the mail box. In all Ernie sent off six letters. But the mails, he knew, were uncertain. So he con-tinued to fashion her replies. At last he wrote down these replies, and he would read them, at home, in the evenings: "My dear friend, you move me greatly." His lips moved as he read. He remembered the phrases in her letters and in his own, and he would go down the street, swinging his right arm and holding his left arm stiff as he hurried along. And the neighbors said, "What can he be talking about to himself that way?"

One night sitting alone by his stove, going over one of her replies, it occurred to Ernie Mendenhall that he was tired of those things that he was saying, as having come from her. What else would she say? He could think of nothing else. Certainly these were rather tiresome—talk about his safety, his loneliness, her coming to Oderhill. Even "My dear friend, you move me greatly" had become tiresome by repetition. Somewhat irritably he saluted the image of her, writing to him, saying to him the same thing over and over. Couldn't she think of anythink else to say?

He began to be bored with her. Feeling the wind blowing in the back of his neck, he asked her quite irritably what had made her leave the window open at the top. Finding the fire low he said to her, in his mind, that she could certainly put in a stick of wood when it was he who filled the wood

box. And when the clock struck a wrong
hour he exclaimed aloud to her that with all
that he had to do, earning their living, he
should have thought that she might wind
the clock. The next morning when he
watered a favorite plant he saw that water
had dripped down on the rosewood melodeon, and he cried reproachfully: "You who
pretended to care for this rosewood melodeon, what have you ever done to protect it?"
But at that she answered quite tartly, and he
was startled and hastened out of the house.

He found that his homecomings had ac-
quired a new fascination. He would come
hurrying into the house and cry: "What?
No fire? No supper? A great way to treat
a man who's been slaving all day for you."
"Slaving indeed!" would come her clear reply. "Writing a few letters for a pittance.
I've a good mind to sell your old rosewood melodeon and make real money for
us." At that he would fly into a rage, and
then grow sullen, and would eat no dinner—actually did eat none; and imagined

Alla Vintrin Mendenhall cooking a steak savory with onions and eating it all alone. Occasionally he would smile at himself awkwardly; but less and less often.

Then a child was born to the writer, and Ernie Mendenhall was extremely shaken. Arriving one morning for work, he heard that faint wailing above stairs. All day when the cry came he could do nothing but listen. And when he went home at night, there was Alla Vintrin Mendenhall with a child.

But now his imagination failed. He had no idea what he would say to her. He could not even look at her. Suddenly she was not there any more, but was wrapt away from him, absorbed in a wailing cry. Sometimes he could catch an outline of her bending head, but when she turned toward him, her face blindingly disappeared and the game stopped. He sat by the stove and imagined her in the room above stairs. He never went there. It was many nights before she was downstairs with him again. He sat making milk toast when she entered.

He looked at her in awe and in silence, but then his milk boiled over on to the griddle and he said: "Is it or isn't it a woman's job to keep things from boiling over, say?" And when he blackened the toast he became fairly caustic. After that they resumed their old quarrels. When she was unconscionably exasperating, Ernie Mendenhall would hurry along the streets, his lips moving as he rehearsed what he would tell her. And the neighbors would say: "Ernie Mendenhall— don't you s'pose he works out puzzles as he walks?"

As the holidays came near, he wandered about in the shops of the little town, thinking of a gift for her and one for the child. But when he touched this or that, it seemed not worthy of them. He bought one little gift, a vase to stand on her melodeon—he thought of it as her melodeon—and on Christmas eve he filled the vase with roses and watched her bend above it, with the child. He thought: "Maybe they meant something like this about Christmas. Maybe it has something to do with somebody being born not of the flesh. . . ." But this he dismissed as unlikely. He prolonged the evening, became involved in dressing an imaginary tree, very tall, and ended in disagreeing with her about having so much tinsel stuff all over everything; found the fire out, and went to bed annoyed by her obstinacy and her carelessness. But he woke once and smelled the roses.

In the holiday week, he came dragging home from his work one dim afternoon, and as he approached his house with its white-laden spruces, he felt a sense of utter weariness at the look of it. At once he knew this as the weariness of the end of a game. He understood that the game had played itself out. All was over, it seemed, the funeral, all; and he entered upon his house as it had been before ever he had seen her. He moved through the little empty rooms, looking at them so differently. Desolation flowed through him. He could experience, but he could not believe that she was gone.

In his mail box waited a letter. Before he opened it he knew her touch. Alla Vintrin wrote: "Dear Sir: Is the rosewood melodeon still for sale? I was married in the spring, and now that we are furnishing our house. . . ." He replied: "Dear Madam: the rosewood melodeon is not for sale. I wish to keep it on account of its associations. . . ." He went into the white night and mailed the letter in the box where he had posted all the others, which she must have received; and he turned back toward the house where she had died.

He had fallen in love, experienced domesticity, been bored by it, and was left alone with the child whom none had ever begotten. He recounted these things to himself as he walked. And the neighbors meeting him said: "Ernie Mendenhall, he's always talking away about something."

THE BIOGRAPHY OF BLADE

"Born in Muscoda. Attended public school in Muscoda. Edited 'The Muscoda Republic' for twenty-five years." Blade had written his biography for the county history. He walked to his home and thought: "It's good. Not many men in the hundred millions are much better off."

He passed the house of Herron, his banker, and heard singing. A woman's voice was singing in a foreign tongue. He walked slowly and listened. In the evening sunlight the banker's house, his lawn, his bridal wreath looked luminous. The air thinned and thickened as cloud and wind wove their uneven ovals. The voice sang on. Blade felt abrupt and obscure happiness. His complacence deepened. "Pretty good. Not many men in the hundred millions are much better off."

Best Stories of 1924; Edward J. O'Brien (Dodd, Mead & Co.).

At his home, about his table, his family
gathered: the woman, all her life of Muscoda, whom he had married; their four
children, contentious, smelling of toilet soap;
his mother, silent and prevalent. His wife,
who seemed to be dining only en route to
real occupation, said:

"Mrs. Herron has asked you and mother
and me to hear somebody sing there to-
night. I can't go; I'm too tired." Without
looking at her, Blade answered, "I'll go to
the Herrons'," and his mother said that she
would go. His wife, going on with her
inner routine, lapsed back into speech with,
"There isn't a thing in the house for breakfast."

About them countless cloudy influences
surged, the melting west, the blue dusk,
heightened sounds from the open. The
room was a theater of airy action. Less
than this were the steak, the apple pie, the
general argument about the pronunciation of
"slough," or, as they rose, that soft flatu-
lence in the throat of his mother. In the

redundant din of dishes, in the clamor of their voices, the faint unearthly splendor died to earthly darkness.

In the night gentle, leisurely, already experimenting with darkness, Blade and his mother went forth. The Herron lawn offered odor of sycamore and wild grape. Blade breathed it, felt happiness, and said to his mother:

"That new county history's coming out. Wonder if you'll like what it says about me." Under the porch lights the fallen muscles of her large face lifted.

In the Herrons' rooms, so regular, so inevitable, the guests gathered. The moquette, the mohair, the mahogany, received them. They were business men and their wives, the accustomed, the dutiful, the numb. There was a rote of jest, of retort, of innuendo. There were the thrilling potentialities and the deathly routine of being. All were tumultuously aware of the little fountain of life within themselves.

At their abrupt, embarrassed hush, Blade

saw near the piano the Herrons' niece.
Her beautiful shoulders, her body cased in
blue, her slow, floating voice, invaded him.
In her he saw and heard all youth, all that
is luminous, all that is different. Upon
Blade invisible hands laid hold. With soft
violence he was claimed, carried, torn.
"What's this?" he felt, and had never felt
so much. For the first time his importance,
his newspaper, his home, his family, were
outdistanced. He saw that this woman lived
in another way than his way, and it was her
way that he wanted.

At the close of her singing, he approached
her. She spoke to him casually, and he
thought that there must be some mistake.
Could she not see that of all those in the
room he it was to whom she had signaled?
He felt that he was crying: "Where are you?
I understand. In God's name, throw me a
rope!" Instead he was saying: "You sing
like a bird, Miss Herron. Much obliged,
I'm sure. I—" When others intervened,
he waited for a long time by the piano, the

stout, smiling man. At length he found his
opportunity, and said to her, "I used to play
second flute myself." But he wondered
whether, after all, he could have said this
aloud, because she only glanced and smiled,
though with that information he had sent
her something vast and pleading. He did
not have another chance to address her.

Out on the street his mother said, "My
dinner didn't set well;" but Blade, in some
powerful onslaught of the unknown, made
no reply and hurried brutally.

He took a blanket and lay on the grass.
There was no change in the trees or the
frogs of Muscoda. There they were, true
to the past. But they were new to Blade,
and so were the stars. It was perhaps the
seventeen-thousandth night of his life, and
yet it was the first. He was feeling: "Say,
music! I've always cottoned to it; but look
what it *is!* Look what it *does!*" Next
door a second-floor window glowed. There
Edgerton, dying, lay expecting to recover.

Every one knew save Edgerton. Blade had
been sorry, but now he was seized and
shaken by the fact that there was Edgerton,
dying and not knowing. With this fact
Blade quivered as occasionally, toward dawn,
he had quivered with remorse or worry.
He experienced Edgerton. Then he experienced delight that he himself was not
dying. The pang of Miss Herron and her
singing returned and returned, powerful,
possessing, and at last excluding.

At daybreak he woke. Long, loose pulsa-
tions of light shook him. Was it light or
was it song? He sat on his blanket and
looked up from the well of his garden to
the sky. He thought: "I'm going to take
music lessons. I'll go and see Miss Herron
to-day, talk with her about it." Countless
cloudy influences surged round the lawn,
where was a theater of changing light and
airy action. For the first time in his life
he saw the morning.

At breakfast his passion for spiritual isola-
tion caused suspicion. "You act as if you're

going to risk some more money," said his
mother. "Better not." And his wife asked
acutely, "What woman was there last night?"
so that Blade thundered, "Can't I have
quiet in my own house?" The children
discreetly tittered. With a wave of nostalgia
it came to Blade that by his words of
thunder he had in some way cut himself off
from Miss Herron. In order to get back
to that world of Miss Herron, he spoke
gently to his wife.

His first act at the office was to request the
return of his biography copy from the editor
of the county history. Blade said, "I can
liven mine up a lot." It had come to him
that he had written a biography which did
not express his life, so rich and so potential.
And now the office routine began—routine,
but yet extraordinary. A pearly shadow
drenched the bare room. Or was it that?
You moved the radio a fraction of an inch,
and you had a new wave length. Blade had
a new wave length. Nothing proceeded in
the old way. The men of the staff of the

composing room, he saw them with incredible intensity, Johns, Lubbock, Mayhew, Platt, in their dirty ticking aprons, with rolled gold rings on the little fingers of inky hands swinging from the elbow. Had Blade ever really seen them until now? He felt in some delicious suspension; or was it balance? Exquisitely rested, he felt, and as if everything were simple. He said to one or two: "Do you know, music is a great thing. For a fact. Wish I'd kept on with second flute that time." He spoke in excitement such that, had they known of a tragedy involving Blade later in the day, they would have remembered. But they did not know of the tragedy.

At eleven o'clock he called the Herrons' house. He waited at the telephone and was rocked on the waves of expectation. A voice came: "Oh, Miss Herron? Oh, Miss Herron left this morning for her home. Who is this calling, please?" Blade mumbled: " 'Muscoda Republic.' Thanks for the item." He groped to the door and stared up and down the street, but she was not passing.

He went at noon to the Muscoda Marble Counter for lunch. The place was clean, the food was good, the women who presided were perfect at their rites. Before the oil-cloth-covered counter Blade sat, and he felt the physical nausea and the shivering of a young animal at night, homeless.

And at night he stayed so long at the office, alone, that Muscoda main street was empty. At his own gate it came to him that he wanted his mother. He was glad that there was a light in her room. He tapped, and sidled toward her, intent on his nameless and infinite loss. Vast and shapeless in her red-and-black checked bath robe, she sat among her plants and bottles and regarded him without change of expression. She commented: "I thought you were going to take me to the picture show to-night." He stood stricken, not by his failure, but by hers. He mumbled and withdrew, and in the passage his wife met him, put her arms about him, whispered, "Nobody loves you as I do!" This should have surprised him, but he was not listening. His soul heard, and cried, "What of it?"

In the night he saw Edgerton's window glowing. Blade felt sorry, an impression now, not an emotion. He woke to the sun and said, "Another fine day," a formula, not a feeling. He went to his office, and the men were pale fellows, inky, disheveled, remote. He faced the blind wall of human loneliness. He was as one who, expecting to be born, is stillborn, and becomes aware not of the cradle, but of eternity.

In a few days Blade appeared before Montgomery, the Muscoda band leader, and said:

"Say, I used to play the second flute myself. And I wondered. . . ."

When "one-night stands" come to Muscoda Opera House, Blade sits in the orchestra and plays the second flute. His detached wife and his grown children come to the Opera House plays, and afterward they ask him why he will deliberately make himself ridiculous by playing in the band. He does not know what to reply and takes refuge in irritability.

In the Muscoda County history Blade's biography, in fine print, stands unread in many little libraries: "Born in Muscoda. Attended public school in Muscoda. Has edited 'The Muscoda Republic' for twenty-five years." To the editor of that history Blade had returned his biography copy without change, and had said:

"I don't know what it was I was going to add. Whatever the item was, it got away from me."

IN THE LOBBY

"This whole love thing isn't enough," said Bruce. "I tell you, it isn't enough."

He stared down the lobby and saw himself on a winter afternoon, fourteen years before, in the street with his two children, and he helpless, so to say, to stem them. When Lois ran ahead, he had quickened his loping step, stooped, and dabbed at her shoulder, apparently unaware that she was unaware of him. He had whirled and threatened, "Come, now!" when little Larry fell behind. One passing could have detected that finding himself alone with these two, Bruce lost his own finished creature-hood, died, rose as their attendant, and existed as an amateur.

One, passing, spoke to her chauffeur and drew to the curb—a dovelike woman, already in a ripening youth, who looked on the children with the look which was intended for Bruce. She said:

"You've not forgotten to-night?"

He had. But remembering, he vowed his remembrance. And Miss Anna Wild, with her brooding way of attention to the children, to him, drove on, with his negative, unconcerned eyes tormenting her, like a positive.

He had gone up one step to his habitable white house, and worked the children into the passage. The passage was right, paneled, discreetly mirrored; the nurse maid was right, by her voice, her eyelids, her quiet, a genius at servitude. When Larry bellowed, "See you to-night, Father," and Lois hit Larry in the head to gain the balustrade side of the stair, this maid hadn't a rebuke; she had: "Only fancy what's for tea." All three vanished.

Bruce had gone into the room where his tea table stood. This room also was right, it rested him as could the cherishing brightness of something happy to think about. But there had been nothing happy to think about, and the very charm of the room had beaten at him like a desire. The whole house had charm; the children, too. But Fanny wasn't there any more, and he was only thirty-six years old.

Overcome by this climax, he had stood staring at his tea table. In a little while Mrs. Beryl would come in and pour. Her cousin would come too, and probably Cory. Cory would hate that hour, and so would he himself. The women would perhaps hate it; only, he thought, they wouldn't know that they did, having known hatred of so much for so long that pretense had now taken its place, unconsidered. But Fanny had loved the tea hour. Had she? Certainly she had. Little thing, in her delicate clothes, living for his love and without another idea—no, no, he didn't mean that; but she *had* loved him. To have lost her after five years of love was ludicrous. He had faced a wall of amazement over which two years had not let him look. From the panels her portrait regarded him, remote, amused. How could she be amused when she was dead, and when he was left here without her and adventureless? He had gone close to the portrait, had remembered her kisses, had her in his arms. He said over her name, "Fanny, Fanny, Fanny." Its reality was a giddiness.

Mrs. Beryl had come into the room, followed by her cousin and Cory. And as he looked into the eyes of the cousin, Lucy Beryl, Bruce had seen that here was a woman whom also he could love.

He had been stupefied, then seized with an excitement beyond anything that he had ever known. Love for Fanny had been the fruit of propinquity. This was the fruit of something else. As strong as his excitement throbbed his sickening sense of guilt. To love some one who was not Fanny? It was even more improbable than had been Fanny's death.

Tea went on. Mrs. Beryl poured, and he had noticed that she powdered her hair so that it should boast of the youth of her face. Her opals had winked like the eyes of a fox.

Having no conversation, she had learned emphasis, and the last word of every sentence escaped her with its vowel trained like a seal. He liked her, laughed at her, looked at Lucy Beryl and trembled. She was as smooth and clear and perfumed as transparent soap. And her little sentences spread from her like lather.

"Can't we have the children in?" Cory had demanded shortly. "Jolly little beggars." Bruce could have embraced old Cory. Bruce wanted to show his children to Lucy Beryl. His children. She did not second the suggestion, and he liked her indifference. Mrs. Beryl said: "Oh, Brucie, do let us! Do-o!" For "o" was such a becoming vowel.

Lois and Larry had come in, and for conduct they dealt in the unbelievabilities, the naïve, the saucy, the devilish, all composed, too, with their courtesy. So far as they had been taught, they were irreproachable; their irregularities lay in their improvisations.

But there was one improvisation for which Bruce had forgiven his Lois.

"Daddy," she said, "are you sad like you look? Larry and I betted. I betted. . . ."

Mrs. Beryl's look enveloped Bruce, appealed to Lucy, and lit on Cory, who crunched a nut.

"They are motherless, the darlings," she explained to Lucy, who blushed. A pretty moment. Mrs. Beryl could not keep her hands off it.

"Go and ask Miss Lucy if she won't tell you a story sometime, lo-vies," she said.

"Know any?" Larry demanded, wheeling on Miss Lucy. "I mean any that are any good?"

"I'm afraid not," said Lucy Beryl. "People always have to tell stories to me."

"Aren't you growned-up?" demanded Lois.

"No," she said, and her eyes danced on Bruce. "Is anybody?" she asked him.

"I hope not," he said gently. He had been enchanted.

"I don't understand children very well, I'm afraid," she said, and Mrs. Beryl looked as if she knew, but was afraid Bruce wouldn't know, that Lucy, from confusion, was lying; but Bruce was thinking merely that this angel was above pretending to swallow his children alive for his sake. Still, when they kissed her as they went away, she did without fervor kiss them rather at large and on the ear; he noticed that. But by then the hour had become, he could recall, a swinging censer whose smoke coursed curling through his veins. When they took their leave, he had gone up to his room and entered it a stranger.

The room was small and sweet and colored. The covers, the linen, the draperies, were of Fanny's choosing. She had liked blue. He stood in the doorway that night and wondered how the room would look in rose.

He had dined alone, and had the children down. He looked at them with anxiety. Lois was six, Larry was five. Soon there

would be for them school, college. Somebody must help them, he was not doing
enough. At dessert he had leaned to them
and admonished them: "You two must be
good—you must be good." When Lois
returned languidly, "Wha' for, Daddy?"
he felt terror. Already was he too late?

He barely remembered his engagement
with Miss Anna Wild, and to keep it, late
in the evening, dragged himself from his
dream. He telephoned her first to ask if
he might still come, heard the patience and
sweetness of her voice, was rested by it. He
thought with pleasure—the pleasure of the
man literally caught away from himself, as
we say, that he would tell her, this old
friend, what had happened to him. Perhaps then he could believe that it had happened, for Anna Wild had known Fanny.
And now the name of Fanny was no longer
a giddiness, but instead seemed to steady
him, or, it might be, rather to take him
aback. He had resolutely repeated the name
Fanny as he walked under the stars.

He remembered that the night had come in a whirl of wind and the cold. Streams of air tore through the darkness, their thin spray switching and stinging, and from inner coverts broke and regathered a thin roar as from some ambiguous beast too old and worn to care to roar. From the core of the cold blew an odor of clean, far plains, tended by the sweep of snow and the killing quality of frost, an odor like the odor of frozen furrows, the pang of spring. Nor was the spring far distant, for already this turmoil was behaving like music, with a recurrent quiet. At such intervals, cloudy spring stars looked on and then withdrew, as if to attend on brighter immediacies. All this came back to him as pungently present as remembered perfume.

Before Anna Wild he had sat down in his tremendous preoccupation. Usually he talked to her about himself. Come to think of it, even though he had been trying to talk of Lucy Beryl, Anna could not have observed the slightest difference. For he

had been telling how Lucy Beryl affected
him. Such had been his conception of talking about Lucy. He had described her by
relating how much he needed her, and had
said, "My children, they are motherless."
Anna had been a receiving station for his
analysis of his own case. He had hardly
seen her plain, dark face, her careful hair.
She was an imperishable-looking lady, and
he had always loved the perishables. "I
wanted to tell you about Lucy Beryl," he
had said lamely. "It is so overwhelming a
thing to feel that I could ever again think
of any woman save Fanny." She did not
say: "You are not thinking of any other
woman. You are thinking of yourself."
She said merely: "Dear old Brucie!" and
he had thought what a brick Anna was. "I
don't know how to get along without you,"
had been his way of expressing his admira-
tion; and she had said dryly that she would
still be there, that it wasn't *she* who had
changed, and had asked after the children.
When she did this the look in her face made

him pause. He could see that look now.
It was a look such as a traveler wears who
faces a memento of home. "Why don't you
adopt a child or two, Anna?" he had asked,
and she had questioned: "Yours?" But he
had said no, that *he* needed them. What
sort of mother would Lucy Beryl make, did
she think? (If he had been as crude in
society as he was on that hearth, he now
thought grimly, he would have been voted
back to pre-cave days before man noticed
that a woman was peering about for a
shelter other than the sky.)

But he had continued to look at Anna.
He had seen her tenderness. He had seen
it turn from the thought of the children to
the thought of him. Afar off he saw, as a
man sees a town where he does not intend
to tarry. He was dazzled, as by a glitter
of sparks which fell from the sky and did
not burn him. Good old Anna!

When shortly he had opened his house
on the sound for a week-end, and had down

Mrs. Beryl and Lucy and Cory, he invited
Anna, in the spirit of unto the least this was
the least that he could do.

On the first afternoon at tea Lois and
Larry were brought in by their admirable
English nurse and handed about like curios.
It was as if he himself had been saying, "I
picked these up with Fanny." They had
behaved as the angels behave, had submitted
to being touched by strange hands, had
looked small and helpless and evanescent,
dancing on the ledge overhanging the abyss
of the past, the future, heredity, hazard, and
diet. The firelight played upon all the
people, made them quick with false motion,
rich with red and orange, drunken with
warmth, and magical with difference. He
remembered that Larry had played with a
little cloth flower, had showed it to Cory,
whom he adored, had whispered to his
father to ask if he might give it to Cory,
had found a box and bestowed on Cory the
flower in an excess of dignity and denial of
self, and then had burst into tears for the

sake of the lost flower. Cory had said, "Oh, I say, old chap, take it back!" Lucy Beryl had cried, "Oh, give him back his flower!" and she had looked beautiful and flushed and indignant as she had folded Larry in her arms. Bruce recalled his enchantment at her bright head bowed above his boy's head. Then he had heard Anna Wild saying:

"Bruce, don't you think it's important not to let him have back that flower? It's really rather crucial for him, isn't it?"

"You're right," Bruce had said, and cried: "Son, you've given away the flower, you know. That's all. . . ."

He saw Lucy Beryl charmingly pout, he saw the quiet power in the face of Anna Wild. And on no more than that cloth flower in his son's hand, it had come to him as by words written in fire on the air that Lucy was no more a mother for his children than a cup of tea, but that Anna Wild was one of those women who mother the very apples on the trees. Mrs. Beryl, who dis-

cerned that her niece was failing, said under
her voice that Lucy was far too sympathetic;
but he saw through Mrs. Beryl as if he had
tasted the blood of a covey of dragons.

His eyes being opened and his ears un-
sealed, he lived through those three days
of the house party like a creature without a
cuticle, raw to every contact. He watched
his new love with his children, saw her spoil
them, puzzle them, tease them, lie to them,
all adorably and damnably. Knowing little
of his children's nervous systems, he learned
much by watching the sportive bombardments
of that beloved, in her play with Lois and
Larry. When he came on her, at dusk,
wrapped in a sheet and telling them a ghost
story, her sweet voice undulating in silvery
wails, he stood stricken. This sheet she
threw from her face, stood meshed in it,
breathless and sparkling, a child, still shud-
dering, circled by each arm. He throbbed
at her presence and winced at her perform-
ance, after an ancient manner in men. On a

pretext he carried the children off, and that night he sat by their beds long after they slept. With social values, with modern values of the individual's motions of duty toward society, Bruce was not much concerned; but the immemorial need of the parent to foster the offspring was in his blood like passion. It was in that hour that he read his own course.

On the station platform, the morning that his house party returned to town, Bruce, as one who has died and is henceforth divorced from earth, watched all those postures, those half looks, those abstractions of Lucy Beryl, and knew that he was seeing them for the last time. By the station door Mrs. Beryl asked him to dine with them on Lucy's last evening, and he accepted, knowing quite well what was hoped of him, knowing too, that he would send some excuse to that dinner and knife a dream, for him already dead or dying. It required days for the dream to die—days spent down in the country alone.

In six months he asked Anna Wild to be
his wife. That was what he asked her, but
what he meant was merely, "Will you be
their mother?" And she knew.

Sitting now with Cory in the lobby of that
Florida hotel, he was thinking of his wife.
She had been to him such a wife as few men
have, he thought, and to his children such a
mother as they had not known even in
Fanny. But he had never loved her; he
had loved Lucy Beryl. And now, after
these fourteen years, with Lois married and
Larry gone round the world, here he was,
at fifty, married to a woman whom he did
not love and never had loved. She had
done an admirable job, but he was bored
by her. And a quarter century of her
stared him in the face.

He tried to think that he was in no worse
case than millions of men, but he admitted
that he was, because with her he never had
known romance. All of romance that he
had seen in his life was still his five years
with Fanny. It was impossible that he

should die in such poverty of experience. He felt richly justified in looking for something else, or so he told himself at that moment. He felt richly justified in his present occupation of looking for Lucy Beryl.

He had deliberately suggested to Anna that they come to Miami, and he had chosen the hotel where he knew that Lucy Beryl lived. He had invited Cory to go, too— Cory who had looked on for fourteen years and, if he had made deductions, had always kept still about them.

This first night in the hotel dining room Bruce had watched the door unceasingly. Anna, plump and content and completely imperishable, looked on, saying nothing, and if she divined, she did not reveal anything at all. She had now the family-off-my-hands look of fifty. Through dinner Bruce had seen her plump throat, the wide parting of her hair, her hand cut by his wedding ring. He thought of Lucy Beryl. If he had married her, his children might now

both be in jail. Or would they? They had
his blood, and Fanny's. Why hadn't he
thought of that in time? And now after
dinner, with Cory there in the lobby, this
thought recurred to him passionately as his
eyes followed Anna, who was looking at the
lobby art. He saw that round head, that
profile tilted estimatingly before a Victorian
waterfall at sunset.

Fourteen years, a quarter of a century to
carry.

The elevator door clicked and slid and
clicked again. From its threshold stepped a
woman in corn color, her light hair bulking
about her ears. She was large, snugly fitted
above the thick, straight waist, slow, very
aware. One might discern at once how,
forty-five years earlier, her baby pictures
had looked.

"There she is," said Cory.

Bruce stared. Unmistakably, there she
was. Lucy Beryl Sanderson, he remembered. And on her track came a drawn man,
with a mothy look, but not from choice.

There she was, his Lucy Beryl, and here was her husband.

With no thought of Cory or of his Anna, Bruce got to his feet and followed not far from the drawn man's side. This man Bruce barely saw. His own eyes were on Lucy, her indolent turn of the head, her ripe shoulders, as smooth as soap. The air of her came back to him, and he breathed it.

The three passed Anna, intent on her Victorian waterfall, her round head tilted appraisingly, now this way and now that. And as they passed her, the drawn man brushed roughly by Bruce, who turned and regarded him, and was stupefied to discern that this man was staring hungrily at Anna, at Anna, who looked so like a dove.

In that instant Bruce could feel himself in the drawn man's shoes, could feel those fourteen years of proximity to this great flaxen Lucy, and those twenty-five years of her to carry. And yoked to Lucy, even as was this drawn man, he saw himself passing Anna, as a stranger in some lobby, and turning to look approvingly at her dovelike presence.

The words which Bruce was framing for Lucy died. He wavered, looked once more at the retreating flax on Lucy's head, once more at her soaplike shoulders. For one moment he breathed her air. Then he wheeled, came back, and sat down by Cory.

"This whole love thing," said Bruce, loudly, "isn't enough. I tell you, it isn't enough."

"Why, no," said Cory. "Of course not."

II

—And Blue

. . . Flowers, pushing through from some inner plane of being, and with such energy that they are visible to man. Especially the blue gentian.

THE NEW BOTANY

THE FOURTH GENERATION

WHEN she was eighty-seven years old, Grandma Imlay's children said that she must not live alone in the winters but must stay with them. Her children were in the sixties, and they spoke with such authority that she obeyed. She stayed for one winter in Bertha's house, and liked it very little, and said so. When spring came she went back with groans and thanksgiving to her little house on the pond, and all that summer she swept the bricks, polished the windows on the inside and fed the birds on the platform of her clothes reel. But when autumn came they had her go to live with another daughter—Emmy. At this compulsion Grandma Imlay made, in her weak way, a furious row, but her row made no difference. They took her away, describing to her how nice and warm she would be. Moreover, Emmy's daughter had just been

married, and she and her husband might as
well live in Grandma's house that winter.

These young people had no wish to begin
housekeeping with Grandma Imlay's furniture, so they stored it in a room of her
little house, and bought new oak. Into her
little linoleum-covered dining room they
moved a huge sideboard and an extension
table; and they took out of her parlor her
center table and her ingrain carpet, and
bought instead a Wilton rug and an overstuffed rocker and divan. Her yellow bedroom furniture they moved to the bedroom
off the kitchen and said that Grandma must
come and stay with them whenever she
liked.

When Grandma Imlay first came in town,
in April, and went to call at her old home,
she trembled with delight to be there again,
where she had lived for sixty-five years.
Here her seven children had been born, and
one had died, here her husband had lived
and died; and she had baked much food
and washed many clothes, had seen her

daughters courted and married, and some of
their children born. There had been little
animals that she had loved, long-ago meet-
ings of her society, boat rides on the pond,
and merry times of house-cleaning and of
holiday. She loved the smell of the lino-
leum and the bare washed boards and the
dining-room table oilcloth.

She entered now upon that oak sideboard
and extension table, the Wilton rug and the
overstuffed rocker and divan. "It's not
the same, no more," said Grandma Imlay.

She went back to her daughter Emmy's.
At first she had been dazed, but when later
she talked of it, her eyes flashed. "I gave
them my house. They took—I don't know
what. No stuff—no. But somethings. It's
not the same, no more."

The young people invited her to come
back and eat with them. She asked, "On
that table?" and said no more. But when
they invited her to come for her birthday,
she went. Some of her old neighbors were
there, young and old. She moved for a

time about the rooms, then went to the door, crying: "Let's go out!" They all sat about on the platform of the clothes reel and on the wash bench and on an overturned tub. She made them bring out there the ice cream and the sunshine cake.

On a day in May they told her that Emmy's grandchild would be born that night, they thought. She said capably: "I will go down there and see what's to be done." When they tried to dissuade her, she said so much that they were obliged to take her there. She went in, and began doing in the old way, and when the nurse and the doctor put her aside, she went out to the platform of the clothes reel and sat there for a long time, not replying. It grew late, and they tried to take her home, but she crept into her kitchen where things were not much changed; and there she waited in the darkness. After a long time she heard the cry of the child. When they brought the baby to the kitchen she sat quiet, and when they showed him to her, she said with no show

of feeling: "Has he got all his arms and
legs?" "Yes, Grandma," they said. "And
he's your first great grandchild." At that
she stared up at them. They left her, counting something on her fingers.

When they were ready to go home she
was not in the kitchen. Emmy thought of
the pond and began to cry: "She's jumped
in the water—she feels she's not needed and
she's jumped in the water!" But then she
opened the door of the bedroom off the
kitchen. There on her old yellow bed-
stead Grandma Imlay was lying asleep. "I
believe," said Emmy, "she's going to stay
here now. What on earth changed her?"

THE QUESTION

Becoming aware that he had no idea
what his life was about, Baldy Michelson
thought that he must end it. How could he
go on with his little grocery and his cement
house on Cottage Grove Avenue, his small
car and his wife? If he had a radio or a
piano player or a child, life might be interesting, or if he could afford to go anywhere for his two weeks' vacation. As it
was, he went for a few days to the Dunes,
then sat at home with his wife or went to
the picture show; and dug in his languid
garden. In the beveled mirror too large
for the bedroom, he saw a man with dead
eyes, expressionless face which did not
change when he spoke. In all his day there
was nothing that he liked to do. Sometimes
he looked at his wife and wondered what
she made of it. But she was a shadow with
a sharp tone.

One day he said to her: "Ella, I can't stand twenty years more of this."

She replied: "Neither can I." It was the first time that they had agreed in years.

He looked at her with new sympathy, saying: "What can we do?"

She said: "Let's sell the house and the business and go abroad."

He cried: "What would we do when our money was all gone?"

She replied: "I don't know, but it would be more interesting than to turn on the gas and leave the money to Alex."

Baldy did not like his nephew Alex either. They sold house, furniture, and business. From the time the hatrack was carried out of the hall, Baldy began to revive.

They bought new clothes, sailed away, saw three capitals, visited the seat of the Michelsons—it was *probably* the same family—and one night were walking in Chelsea when Baldy said:

"How'd it be to buy a nice villa over here

and settle down? I was talking with the greengrocer yesterday. He needs a partner. . . ."

They bought the villa in Chelsea, a small car, and hoped to have a radio or a piano player, but not yet. When vacation came they went for three days to Brighton. When they returned Baldy dug in a languid garden, went to the cinema and sat at home with his wife. In five years he looked in their beveled mirror and saw himself with dead eyes and unchanging face; and in a voice which did not change either he said to his wife: "Ella, how would you like to go back to the States?"

She replied with emotion: "Let's go, let's go!"

They sold the villa and the greengrocery partnership, and when they arrived in Chicago, Baldy found that his former partner was getting on and wished for some help. So they rented a house on Cottage Grove Avenue, and Baldy went back to that grocery.

"This is something like!" cried Baldy, and his wife thought so too.

Five years later he saw in the mirror an aging man,. with dead eyes, who spoke in a dead voice. His partner was old, his wife was an icy shadow; and if only they could go somewhere for a vacation or could afford a radio or a piano player. . . .

"We had it nice in Chelsea," said his wife.

"We did," he agreed, thought of the greengrocery, Brighton Beach and the cinema, and said: "Ella, I can't stand ten years more of this."

They were sitting on the side porch and Baldy stood up and shook his fist at the evening sky.

"What's it *for?*" he shouted. "That's what I don't sense. It ain't in the game to give a man a brain and then not tell him what it's *for.*" He looked at his wife, his dead eyes unchanging, and said in his flat voice: "Ain't there *anything* that could tell

a person what it's for?" But she had no
answer.

That evening Alex unexpectedly arrived.
Baldy never had liked Alex, a little man,
with an eager manner and no great respect
for business.

"I dropped in," said Alex, "to take you
both over to my camp for Sunday. Can
you go?"

"*Your* camp?" said Baldy, and felt a new
respect for Alex. Had he struck a good
thing?

They drove to a corner of the forest
reserve where were lines of gray ghostly
tents and a living eye of fire in the midst.
Around the fire were fifty boys, one boy
standing before them. Alex and Baldy
Michelson and Ella Michelson sat on the
edge of the company and listened:

"We've all had the week here, fellows,"
came the hesitant voice, "and we could have
another one. But there's fifty that ain't
going to get to camp at all, 'count not money
enough. What do you say we start going

back and give the other fifty their chanst?"

There came groans and hisses. But they took the vote, counted hands, and the vote was to let the other fifty come out.

"Nice kids," said Alex to Baldy. "Never had a thing, either. But they've got the gang sense—the whole gang, I mean. They never saw one of these fifty boys they're giving up their week for, you understand."

"The whole gang," Baldy repeated. "What's that?"

Sitting among them on the Sunday, their last day in the camp, Baldy said to his wife: "Ella, they're got hold of something or other. So has Alex. . . ."

She returned vaguely: "Do you think so?"

That night, as they were falling asleep, Baldy said: "Ella! I'll bet Alex staged that, thinking I'd put up for the extra two weeks of camp for those boys. I never thought of that. . . ."

She said sleepily: "Oh, surely not, Baldy. Alex isn't crazy."

"All the same, he's got hold of something or other," Baldy muttered.

He went to his grocery. Mrs. Michelson tidied the house. At night they went to a picture show. In time they bought a piano player and a radio. They often sat on the side porch at evening and Baldy would shake his head and say: "What's it all for?   That's what I don't sense."

But when he died, he left his money to Alex. "Because," Baldy explained to his lawyer, "I think he seems to have got hold of something. . . ."

THE VOICE

BASSET had engaged passage on the *Titanic*, for her first crossing. Any one sailing at that time would have done the same, providing he could still get passage. Basset was delighted at the promise of the swift luxurious voyage, and he said to his friends:

"I'm off—on the *Titanic*—yes. Better come along."

He cabled his financée and his firm, said his farewells and did his final shopping.

He was walking in Regent Street when he first became aware of a faint impulse within him, less than a force, more than a fragrance; an impulse to cancel his passage. At first he did not notice, and when his urge did break through to his consciousness, he understood that it had been beating at him for a long time. As soon as it was definitely noticed, it became a clear and clamorous command.

He argued the matter with this inner disturber. Cancellation was impossible. His arrangements were all made, invitations had been refused, his cables had been sent, and Marie would be counting the days. There was now no earlier boat and he was averse to all postponements. In reply to all this came three distinct words:

"Cancel your passage."

Now Basset was accustomed to obey this inner impulse. He hadn't an idea what it was, and in general he thought if you classified a thing you had disposed of it. But though he called this voice the subconscious, he continued to obey it, secretly and blindly, but pretty consistently. And the more often he obeyed it the more pressing it became, until, as now, having listened, he could not dismiss it.

So he canceled his passage, sent off two more cables, and tucked himself into the cabin of an old liner sailing a day later. He was on the deck of this old liner when he was told of the message from the *Carpathia,* crying the *Titanic's* fate.

Shaken by the disaster, he was yet kindled by the memory of what had occurred. He had been saved—but how? Unquestionably he could not be the only one to whom this saving voice had spoken. There must be people on this very boat. . . .

He went among the passangers and asked them, nakedly, if they had had a like experience. From a passenger list of seventy, he found six who had taken passage and given it up for a similar reason and eleven who had thus been prevented from taking passage at all.

"Then why," he shouted to a woman who had held her *Titanic* passage for a month, "why were *they* not given this impulse—the people who sailed?"

"Perhaps they were," said this woman, "and they didn't listen."

When his boat had docked and he kissed Marie, exceedingly smart and very tender, she cried: "Oh, my darling—thank God you changed your passage. How did you come to do that?"

Basset told her, reluctantly, feeling a sense of exposure. At once upon her arrival at home she repeated the story to her family, in his presence. At dinner that night she made him tell it again. The newspapers came and interviewed him on it, and then his firm associates questioned him minutely—"No, but, just exactly how did the voice sound?"—and at his club they made him tell it again and again, and there they began to joke to him about it.

A woman's association asked him to come and speak informally on his wonderful, wonderful metaphysical experience, and he was drawn into an acceptance; and goaded too far by their awe, he informed them that this was the most usual thing in the world; that he had been obeying this inner voice for years, and that they could all do the same if they were not too battered by—"by tea and cakes," he told them rudely.

"But what *is* it?" they wanted to know.

"It's conscience," he said bluntly, "working as it was intended to work. Also, it's electricity. If we could raise our consciousness high enough, we'd always have this kind of thing. . . ."

Now the scientists attacked him and demanded to know what on earth he meant by electricity, and the psychologists what on earth he meant by higher consciousness and universal substance, and the theologists what on earth he meant by dragging conscience into the routine of the market place? The weekly reviews and the daily headlines took up and tossed about Basset and his inner voice. He thought: "I shall lose my power. It is not that they have cut my hair. All the same, they have shorn me."

He fled to a mountain camp and one day went out alone in a canoe on a mountain lake. As he pushed off, he distinctly divined an agonized command not to step into the canoe. It upset, in the green and glossy water. A guide heard his cries and came running and shouting as the waters closed over Basset's head.

THE WOMAN

WALKING one day in a suburb, Bellard, wearing clothes in the extreme of the fashion, was torn by the look of a house on whose mean little porch near the street sat a shabby man of sixty, without a coat, and reading a newspaper. The man's fate seemed terrible: the unpainted house, the disordered hall, the glimpse of a woman in an apron. But the man looked up, and smiled at Bellard as brightly as if he himself had been young.

Bellard meant to be a financier. Instead, he shortly endured his father's bankruptcy, left college, found uncongenial employment, observed the trick of a girl's eyes, married her and lived in a little flat.

But this girl had the quality of a flower. Bellard could not explain it, but she was silent and fragrant, and hopeful like a flower. Once in April when he saw a pot of lilies of the valley blooming on the pavement, he thought: "They're like Lucile. They're all doing their utmost." In her presence it was impossible to be discouraged. He would go home from work hating his office, his routine, his fellows, his street; but as soon as he entered the flat, there would be some breath of that air for which he saw other men dying. Her welcome, her abstraction, her silence, her confidences were all really heavenly. Bellard wondered at her, did not comprehend her, adored her. He worked hard, and went home on the subway with a sense of happiness.

He longed to give her beautiful things, but she said: "How did people get like that, my dear—to want expensive things and to have people look up to them? Isn't it foolish?" He wondered how she knew that, and he wished that he knew it himself.

Their two children were like all agreeable children, and Bellard and Lucile went through the reverence, anxiety and joy of their upbringing. And whether the moment yielded a torn frock or a hurt knee, croup or a moral crisis, Lucile seemed to put the event in its place and not to be overwhelmed by it. "She has a genius for being alive," Bellard thought.

As she grew older, she was not so beautiful, and he saw many women both beautiful and young. But when they chattered, pouted and coquetted, when they were cynical, bored, critical, or hilarious, he thought about Lucile and her silences, her fragrance, her hope. Hope of what? She knew that they would in all probability never have any more than they had now. When he asked her wistfully what kept her so happy she replied with an air of wonder: "You."

One day he overheard her talking about him with a friend. Lucile was saying: "Other men live in things and events and emotions and the future. But he seems to know that living is something else. . . ." "What else?" this friend interrupted curiously. And he heard Lucile say: "Well, of course every one knows, really. But he lives it too."

"I'm not good enough for her," Bellard thought, and tried his best to prove that he was.

They went on like this for years; the children grew up, married, came home and patronized them. Then Bellard, who had established a little business, failed. His son tried to straighten things out, found it impossible, and assumed control, frankly berating his father. His daughter came home with her three children, and filled the flat with clamor and turbulence. This woman said: "Mother, sometimes I think it's your fault. You're so *patient* with him." "I'm glad he's out of that business," said Lucile absently. "He never liked it." Her exasperated daughter cried: "But what are you going to live on?" Bellard heard her say: "Your father was responsible for three of us for a quarter of a century you know, dear." At this Bellard rose on strong wings and felt himself still able to breast the morning and the night.

Lucile and Bellard moved to a suburb. There they rented a little house and Bellard

went into a real estate office. All day he
showed land and houses to men who wanted
something better for less money. At night
he went home and there was Lucile—less
like a flower, but still silent, fragrant, hopeful. He said to her: "You'll never have
anything more than you have now, Lucile,
do you realize that?" She replied: "I don't
want anything more to dust and take care
of!" Once he said: "When you were a girl
you dreamed that you'd have things different,
didn't you, Lucile?" She said: "My dear,
all that poor girl knew how to dream was
just about having things!" He cried: "What
do you want most of anything in this world?"
She considered and answered: "I want you
to be as happy as I am."

He thought of his own early dream of
being a great financier, and said: "I'm the
happy one, you know." He thought: "This
is what the world is dying for."

One day, when he was sixty, he was
sitting on his mean little porch near the
street. The house was small and unpainted,

the hall was disordered with house cleaning,
Lucile in an apron was in the doorway. Bellard, without a coat and reading a newspaper,
lifted his eyes, and saw walking by the house,
and wearing clothes in the extreme of the
fashion, a youth who looked up at him with
an excess of visible compassion.

On this youth Bellard looked down and
smiled, a luminous smile, a smile as bright
as if he himself had been young.

A FAR CRY

Among the red porch chairs Elmer Dasher sat in a denim swing which leniently dissented. He did not seem like a man who would sit and swing; such a molested-looking man.

Hands parted the curtains of a window behind him and hung there a pink card on which was printed "Ice." It was evening, but to-morrow morning's slumber must not be flawed by this task. Immediately the hands appeared upon the porch. Mrs. Dasher's hands wore all the expression that she had. They seemed to have done so much. Her face had experienced so little.

"Hot," said she.

"Why shouldn't it be? It's summer time," said Elmer Dasher.

He tilted the swing, and the spirited disclaimer of the frame did not annoy them. She rocked and they did not hear the creak-

ing board. Near the cement pavement the
sprinkler fizzed and spurted; they did not
observe that in order to avoid it, passers were
obliged to make a detour under the maples.

Elmer Dasher took his watch and held it.
The last bright cloud hung on Patch Hill
and stained the air. Shadow floated and
fell. For five minutes while airy dissolu-
tion ran upon the light, Mr. Dasher eyed
the dial. Then he descended the steps and
turned off the city water. Unconscious that
it was a triumph of social evolution for a com-
munity to be organized like that, and without
a casual glance at the elemental glory of
the sunset, he returned to his swing.

Ludlow, his neighbor, crossed the connect-
ing lawns and desired to know how everything was. Ludlow had a woman's eyes.
Elmer Dasher held him in subconscious con-
tempt, for he made disconcerting observa-
tions, such as he made now to Dasher's inevitable reply that everything was complete,
complete:

"Sometimes I wonder why Patch Grove

doesn't collapse and slide down Patch Hill
and pile up in the valley."

Dasher inquired why on earth it should
do that. He knew his town; "hard-boiled
business, hard-boiled recreation, hard-boiled
family life," he had once summed it up;
but he could not imagine why business blocks,
houses, garages, and folk should ever give
way, of their own futility, and slide down to
the valley of the Patch, the brown river.
Ludlow's long harangue only confused him.

"You won't find any better place to live,"
he indignantly defended. "I'm afraid not,"
said Ludlow, sighed, mentioned the thunder
heads in the west, and went home.

"Queer duck," Elmer Dasher thought.

Abruptly, distinctly, he heard a cry. He
could not divine its direction nor tell whether
it was the voice of man or woman. It might
have been a signal, very clear, though from a
distance. He looked at his wife but she, with
moving lips, was counting something and
had heard nothing. He thought that the

boys must be playing ball on the school grounds, and he tilted the swing again.

The hall gas flared up. Over her who had lighted it the warm tide surged, showed her pointed face, her thin arms—Geraldine Dasher, a name to which her faint self of forty bore no relation. She emerged, announced a destination, was met by "Why not ever sit down here at home with us?" and pregnable, without resentment, sank to the top step.

Within the houses, behind the dying brilliance of the brick walls, girls were dressing. In Patch Grove no one dressed before dinner. The virginity of the toilette was preserved for its main purpose. On the porches sat those who did not dress for the evening any more. In many of these the desire to give life had changed to a dynamic hostility to those already alive. As with the Dashers:

"Hot." "Why shouldn't it be? It's summer time." "That isn't funny." "My dear, nothing is funny to you." "My clothes are —they're so funny I don't like to go to church." "The churches have gone to the dogs. Best keep out of them." "You would insult my religion!" And so on to: "I'm rather sick of this whole thing." Whereon Geraldine cried abruptly: "How do you think I feel about that?" and laughed harshly, so that a silence fell.

In their silence a telegram was given over the telephone in the hall. Dasher took the message, came back, his face sagging with concern, and said:

"Mamma, Katy's sick. She wants us to go to the city and bring the boy home with us."

Mrs. Dasher asked for details which had not been given, made and rejected fractions of plans, objected. Dasher said: "Nonsense. Katy's the only niece I've got in the world. Going, too, Jerry? Don't keep us waiting."

The enormous night received the little car. Ten miles of dusky cornland, warm with the breath of the day; eight miles of city streets, sleepy with heat, nervous with light, washed by a thin black stream of beings, Pearl City traffic formed the veins of some

vast undivined body. That body seemed to
have a voice, raucous, unresting. The powers
of that body were evident—to give death, to
give life, to sin, to rejoice, to agonize. Was
there no more to that unknown being? Could
it only bellow with its body while its veins
flowed with the traffic?

Katy was at a hospital and with her the
little boy, wondering, frail. The ward was
shared with a woman, a Bohemian, red and
black. Katy was a yellow shadow on a pillow. Old in cell and in spirit she said:
"Don't bother to stay. He'll be here. But
he can't work and see to the boy, too. Me?
I don't know and I don't care." She lay like
a little animal left too long in a trap to be
watching any more.

Elmer Dasher was shaken, said, "But my
God, Katy"; and Katy, turning her head fret-
fully from him, was caught by the aspect of
the Bohemian woman, and cried out. The
Bohemian woman was sitting erect and trying
terribly for breath. No nurse was there, the
passages were quiet. The Dashers, always

lax, uncentered, were thrown into distraction. Elmer ran and rang and called. It was Mrs. Dasher who reached the woman and, in some deep impulse to physical contact, held her as she died. Mrs. Dasher kept saying: "I don't understand this. I don't understand this."

Jerry caught up the terrified little boy, ran by the nurse who was moving upon the room, crouched in the tonneau, and hugged the child. He wept, was stilled, and later roused to faint interests. She was stirred by his quiet, then by his motion. While they waited, she sought for ways to give him protection. Passers glanced at them and it flashed to her: They think he's mine. She adjusted his collar and said in an admirably imitated abstraction: "Yes, darling."

At last her father and mother came crossing the street. To Jerry they seemed detached and of a familiarity strange and passionate, such as she felt in saying over her own name.

"I don't understand that," Mrs. Dasher

was still saying weakly. In the seat beside her husband she wept and seemed rapt, unaware of anything save that which had just happened. Elmer Dasher was silent, but wholly in the body, as was clear when he cursed in a traffic crisis.

This crisis he assumed to have been imagined: He heard a car, with a strange siren, a faint melodious siren; a car seeking, he thought, to pass him, and nearly succeeding. Dasher could hear the silver alternation, a cadence such as three pipes might give, softly blown. When had a man ever devised a siren like that? "Some music hound," thought Dasher. And when a tight place narrowed in before him and the light cry of insistence followed close, he drew far to the right to let the fellow pass. The fellow did not pass. Amazed, as he looked back, Dasher saw the street momentarily empty. "Must have been the fire whistle," Dasher thought, swore, and slid back into the channel.

They drew into the country, into the tender vacant air of fields. Now emerged the sky, which in town they had forgotten. The sky was void of stars. To the southwest were thrusts of lightning, incessant, at innocent play, unconcerned with any fruit of death. A faint huskiness came deepening, of thunder.

"What's that?" the child asked and, grown shyly accustomed, questioned of fireflies, of miasma, of the smell of honey and hay. These questions gave Jerry rapture. His breath and his brushing eyelash gave her rapture. The child fell asleep, and in dear discomfort Jerry held him; for mile upon mile she held him and dreaded the ride's end.

She felt a lift of pleasure when the car was stalled. At the foot of a sharp slope up to a roadbed the car stopped. Elmer Dasher, who could not so much as set a hinge on a door, was helpless. He lifted the hood, produced tools, said names of parts; but it was plain that he was helpless. No farmstead light was near and they set themselves to wait for passers. It was a road little fre-

quented. And now the high black clouds
were shot with flame.

They faced a meadow made limitless by
night. The life of the dark was there, the
dark peopled by rustle, breath, odor. In the
stillness these influences came confidently to
the car. The night breathed, and along its
vast invisible veins coursed some faint fluid,
tincturing the darkness, flowing through the
little bodies of men.

Suddenly Elmer Dasher felt a frightful
nostalgia. Home, home! He wanted to be
at home. But when he thought of his house,
his porch with red chairs, it was not these
that he wanted. Home. Some core of the
world seemed to emerge and demand him.
Where did he want to go?

Far away, as if from another meadow
under another night, there came a call, of
no remembered bird. A bird call which fused
with the rising wind, threaded the thunder,
haunted the ear, and died. It voiced his nostalgia, it was pure and pleading. It bore
an echo of unbearable sweetness. Or was it

a bird call? He thought now that it might have been a wavering engine whistle. . . . Far down the curve of the railroad across the distant swamp, a yellow eye outrayed in the first rain.

"The 'way freight," said Elmer Dasher. "It's none too good for us. We'll signal them, and if they row we'll report them to the directors!"

The highway was level with the fields. To the fields' edge they rolled their car, an ancient servant, and left it locked in darkness; with its lamps they lighted their way and flagged the freight train. In magnificent languor, like a train of the Orient, the thundering thing rolled indolently down and stopped. A blown torch brushed out a little pool of light. A Patch Grove voice hailed them, exclaimed, bade them climb aboard. Received into the warm cave of the cab, these four blinked at the red throat of the firebox and felt the rich reprieve of some convalescence.

The enormous night held the little train.

The enormous sky held the little storm. Standing in the gangway Elmer Dasher threw back his head and took the hour. Motion, roar, electricity blue on the metal, thunder of wheel and of cloud, and he in their midst. He felt in flight over farther spaces. They swept by a steel plant, saw the belch and glare, made out men and mounds of slag. One of the sheds stood drenched in the red beauty of the pouring, and naked figures flowered from wild color. In that flash were the tumult of farther industry, roar of innumerable trains, glitter of all the cities, their veins flowing with men and women in sin, joy, anguish. He was feeling all that there was to feel! He could have cried a challenge as the engine went challenging the lit blackness.

But why did the engineer blow the whistle, running through open country? Or *did* he blow the whistle? He was sitting quietly on the seat, his attention on the track. One hand lay on his knee and one on the windowsill. The engine whistle was not blown! That insistent call that seemed like the voice of their flight, it came toward them from some horizon. What horizon? Who was calling? Calling whom? Beauty and anguish flowed together in Elmer Dasher. He felt drunkenness, incredibly enhanced.

"The glory of the Lord—eh, old girl?" he shouted. No one heard him.

On the fireman's seat Mrs. Dasher, cowering with covered eyes, looked round at him. She had not heard what he said, had not seen what he saw, had felt nothing that he felt, had been puzzled by no cry; but her face held its own emotion, wore now as much experience as her hands.

"Elmer," she cried, "I don't understand what happened to her and I don't believe I ever shall."

But this he did not hear. "The glory of the Lord, by the great horn spoon!" he bellowed, and looked about.

Neither death nor the fury of the hour occupied Jerry. In the thunder of the engine and of the storm, she had found that the child clutched at her.

Before midnight they were dry in their rooms and the little boy was sleeping. Elmer Dasher's exaltation, his wife's pity and terror, Jerry's brief motherhood, all boxed dry in their rooms.

The storm cleared and left the air sultry, intolerable. Dasher could not sleep. He went downstairs and sat in the swing. Ludlow was moving about the lawn, barefooted in the drenched grass. He came to the Dasher's verandah rail.

"Been up in town, have you?" he said. "I tell you, if there's a reason why Patch Grove should collapse and slide into the valley, Pearl City ought to drop into the ground with no warning. Ought to disappear from the human eye."

Something shook Elmer Dasher. He seemed to remember that this destiny of man he had recently been stirred to resist. But automatically he replied:

"You won't find a better city anywhere than Pearl."

"I'm afraid not," said Ludlow, and went home.

Faintly, a far horn which would wake few, Elmer Dasher heard the cry again. In it was the nostalgia of the night, of the world, of some hidden being striving to be heard. But of this cry he could not divine direction or meaning. It might have been a signal or a challenge. To whom? And from where? Boys could not be playing ball on the school grounds now. . . .

He moved nervously in his swing and the frame dissented leniently. He felt an instant and acute relief and comfortably concluded that this faint squeak was all that he had noted.

Hearing this squeak, his wife descended, quavered. "That you, Elmer?" and came to her rocking chair on its creaking board. The moon in its third quarter, a trinket of silver gilt, was tilted above the elm, but the Dashers did not observe. Nor did they note the clean new anger of the second storm cutting its low way along the west.

Beneath the hall burner Jerry passed, came to the threshold, and when her mother said "Better sit down," emerged and obeyed.

"I don't understand it and I never shall," said Mrs. Dasher heavily.

"Don't say that again!" Elmer Dasher cried. "There isn't a woman in the world that'll keep on saying the same thing over and over the way you will."

"I won't be here long to say anything. I'm sick of the whole thing."

Jerry interposed: "It's hot again, isn't it?" She heard: "Why shouldn't it be? It's summer time." And: "Can anybody see whether I hung up the ice card?"

THE TWO SOULS

Marthella brought to the kitchen table a five-pound jar of butter and six butter pats, white bread, devil's food, filled cookies. In the woodshed Malcolm had already ranged the boxes of potatoes, tomatoes, grapes, the two squashes, the tray of "mixed" vegetables. All their entries were ready for the County Fair.

Malcolm came in, stamping. On the other end of the kitchen table Marthella had ready their two plates, coffee cups, soup bowls. She carried steaming soup to his plate. Then she sat down in the high-backed rocking chair near the red hearth. She had spent a difficult day. The last straw had been that Millie, her little maid, had asked to go home for the rest of the week. Marthella thought angrily that she shouldn't go home.

"Have you eaten?" Malcolm inquired,

then noted the unused dishes at her plate. "Aren't you going to eat anything?"

He almost never called her Marthella any more, nor did she call him Malcolm.

"I'm so tired," she said, "I can't eat."

"So am I," he said testily, "but I've got sense enough to eat, anyway."

"Some folks are all sense . . . one kind," she retorted tartly.

"I'd have more of the other kind if you were as saving as some," he returned.

At this Marthella fell to quiet weeping.

He took his soup in silence and presently remarked:

"I'll bet Sims gets first on his mixed vegetables. My 'bagies aren't up to his. Sims is an old snide," he added, his face hardening and sharpening. "He can't farm for sour grapes. But he can bluff."

Still weeping, she said:

"If any of my stuff gets first, you keep the money. I couldn't touch it. It'd burn me."

She knew that she could "touch" it, and he

knew that he would not take her first-premium money. But he replied indifferently:

"All right. It can go toward the milking machine."

Marthella ceased weeping. Two red spots burned on her cheeks. "I was going to use it toward the parlor carpet," she said. "But I don't care how the parlor carpet looks. Nobody sees it."

"No," he assented. "Nobody. Nobody but you."

"Yes. I'm nobody," she contributed.

He said nothing.

"I'm going to paint the kitchen floor," he announced after an interval. "I think I'll paint it brown."

"Because brown's hard to take care of?" she inquired. "And yellow's easy?"

He burst into laughter. "I did that to try you," he told her. "Last time I said 'yellow,' and you said yellow was calf color and you wanted brown. Just plain cantankerous, you are."

Stung by the injustice of this, her voice rose shrilly:

"I didn't know brown was hard to take care of then, did I? Well, I know now, because I've had it. And I say I want yellow."

He continued to laugh, rose, pushed his chair under the table, then leaned upon it.

"We'll start," he said, "before six in the morning. I want to get a good place for my stuff."

"You can start when you like," she replied. "I'm not going."

And this she heard herself say exactly as if some one else had said it, with whom she had no traffic. The words amazed her. She had not meant to say that. She had meant to go to the Fair. She had not missed a Fair in thirty years. She had spoken without her own will, and now she knew that she must live up to her declaration.

"I may not be able to spare a team to go in again this week," he reminded her.

"I shall not go in again this week," she

said with deliberation. "I shall not go to
the Fair at all."

At least she enjoyed the sensation that she
was making. He knew that she was not given
to speaking lightly. Having said that she
should not go, Marthella, as he had come to
know her, would not be going.

"Suit yourself," he said only, and went to
the barn.

Marthella sat in a web of silence—an
abrupt accusing silence. What had she done?
She had taken away her chief pleasure of the
year, when she met friends not seen year-
long. Also she had forgone her premium
money, which came to her every year, and
was her only money to spend as she liked.
Why had she done this? To satisfy something which even now was taking satisfaction,
as a beast of prey, over some bleeding victim.

Who was that bleeding victim?

She was hungry, but she sat without eating,
as if this were a part of that same savage satisfaction. She looked at the red coals of the

hearth. How very bright they were! How very bright they were!

The door opened and her husband came in. He sat opposite to her, before the hearth, and stretched his feet to the fire. He, too, stared at the red coals on the hearth. She looked at him. He was very bright and shining.

There he was, Malcolm, as she knew him, but shot through with some incalculable cast of radiance. His face was serene and beautiful—not as she remembered it in his youth, not as she might imagine it in death, but all compounded of both, and majestic beyond the faces of men.

He spoke to her in the voice that she knew, but keyed now to something gentle.

"Have you got any salve?" he asked. "I seem to have hurt myself."

She rose and went to the cupboard. As she returned she saw herself in the mirror above the wash bench: her tired face, her smooth hair, her open collar. And she was as luminous as he.

There was no time to think of this. She went to him with the salve, stooped to him. He lifted his hand, with a gesture like that of a little child. She touched him.

And from her to him, and from him to her, went some flow of power which filled the room. Not power which shook them. But something which seemed to have been there for a very long time.

She went back to her chair and they talked. And all the time she looked breathlessly at this being. Was it Malcolm? Had he died, and had this one come instead? But what of her? She glanced down at her blue dress. It seemed clean and soft, and its fabric was like silk. Her hands, too, were smooth and lay unwontedly disclosed. And all was shining. . . .

He had his head on the chair back in a way that she knew.

"We ought to get the kitchen papered," he was saying.

"I wish we could," she answered. "Some of the pretty, cheap paper—plain, maybe."

"Yes, cheap," he assented. "I don't know as I always fancy plain paper——might show the dirt more. Would it?"

"Perhaps it would," she said. "We could tell when we came to pick it out."

He agreed. "I guess we better see about that when we get a chance. We'll go to Sims' for it."

"Sims' is the best place," she assented. "Sims hasn't been out here in quite a while," she added.

"I wish't he'd come," Malcolm said heartily. "There's nobody does me more good than Sims. But then, he's always doing somebody a good turn. As he did Elder."

"The one he found sleeping in the hay," she recalled.

He nodded. "The ex-convict," he said. "Gosh, think of it! College and all that, and not a friend when he came out. He's been a son to Sims."

Some exquisite current of feeling ran through Marthella. It made her both faint and divinely strong. Her eyes were on Mal-

colm; and now, as she saw him smiling with
his joy in Sims, and expressing that joy, his
body was pulsing with more light, like a soft
sun. She looked down at herself. Was she,
too, brighter?

She wondered what would happen next.
She felt a sense of perfect happiness, as at
the onset of some gentle force, which entered
and held her and would not let her go. She
must try to speak it.

"Millie wants to go home for the rest of
the week," was what she said. "Her sister
is there. I'm going to let her go. I can get
along."

And at this she was aware that her own
being was bathed in a fairer shining.

He assented. "Millie's a nice little thing,"
he added. "I wish't we could do something
for her."

She leaned forward eagerly.

"Oh, Malcolm!" she said. "I've got some
things I could fix up for her, if—do you
s'pose we could send her to school? Some
little place?"

Until that moment she had never thought of this, but the plan seemed to rise within her, full-formed.

"If that's what we'd rather do," he answered. "I've been thinking—we ought to pick out some few things like that and then go to work and do them."

He spoke with a manner of hesitation, almost of surprise . . . as if, say, he were trying to remember when he had thought of this.

"Oh, let's!" she cried. "And Millie'll be one of 'em. I'd put the premium money in."

She tried to remember what had been said, of late, about that premium money. Something that hurt her, somewhere. But she had forgotten. In any case the money should go to Millie.

Malcolm rose, and the brightness which was he moved as he moved, and she looked up at him with wonder.

He crossed to the clock and wound it. She could see the turn of his arm and his huge

hand, could hear the regular scrape of the
weights as they rose to his touch.   And yet
he was as lucent as an angel: the old blue coat,
the rough hair, the worn shoes—all.

She looked about on the objects of the
room.   Everything stood in some exquisite
change.   The clock shelf, the mirror, the
wash bench—what homely graciousness, what
dignity!   As if their delicate offices of telling
the time, reflecting, cleansing, were upon
them like visible garments.

The cupboard, with one door ajar—she
knew those dishes within so that a crack, a
nick, was an event.   Yet there they stood, in
some delicate difference, vessels of still fur-
ther ceremonial.

And this was true of the window, looking
on the mystery and the splendor of the night.
And of the hearth, red with fire, mystic and
very bright.   And on the table waited the
work of her hand, to be taken on the morrow
to the County Fair.   There they were, the
elements of the body, in their mantle of per-

fection, ready to be blessed, as for some secret sacrament.

All this was to her but a current of feeling, deep, glad. She thought about the Fair, that assembling of the people, people whom she had known from her girlhood; greeting, laughter, music, hands. . . .

She thought about the County Fair ground, and it seemed to be swimming in this brightness which enveloped Malcolm and her.

He closed the clock door, and turned.

"Come, Marthella," he said. "We must get a pretty good start in the morning."

Had some one, sometime, laid upon her that she was not to go to the Fair? She hardly thought of this. She was smiling, because he had called her by her name.

What a wonderful thing a name was, within! Marthella! It seemed to her new, like another name. A name which was in itself a woman. She rose to be that woman. All this was to her merely as gladness.

"Yes, Malcolm," she said.

He fastened the door, blew out the lamp,

and there were the coals on the hearth, very, very bright. . . .

Together they groped to the stair door, and that homely way received them, as if abruptly it came forward to perform its authentically appointed service. And there in the stair-way that brightness followed. It was in their chamber, mingling with the moonlight. The white curtains, patterned with the moving leaves without, the familiar objects of gloom and light—all there stood in some robing, some dignity of their simple offices.

And when had there been in the house this indeterminate perfume. . . .

They undressed without a lamp—there was no lamp in the chamber. They lay down in that tender, engulfing tide. Sleep came, and as it came there beat about them the sense of some besetting sweetness, but strong with the strength of that force which had seized upon them at birth and had caused them to live.

In the morning, as they drove away from their door, the first sun came slanting along